Dawn Of the Cicada.

By E.A. Green

Published through Jack in The Green Publishing.

Copywrite © 5-27-2019 E.A. Green

All rights reserved.

No part of this book may be reproduced, stored in a retrieval system, or transmitted in any form or by any means without the prior and written permission of the publishing author, except by the reviewer who may quote brief passages in a review to be printed in a newspaper, magazine or journal.

!WARNING!

This is a graphic novel with extreme language, adult and sexually explicit situations involving taboo subject matter which deals with the illegal acts concerning certain fictional characters.

At no time does this author condone such illegal acts that are only being used to describe a character's actions relating to this work of fiction.

TABLE OF CONTENTS.

CH 1.
WHEN THE APPLE IS RIPE.

CH 2.
FABUOUSLY DELICIOUSE.

CH 3.
JOHN AND MARY SITTING IN A TREE.

CH 4.
PLAY BALL.

CH 5.
APPLE SAUCE.

CH 6.
DUDLEY, DUDLEY, DUDLEY.

CH 7.
DON'T SIT UNDER THE APPLE TREE.

CH 8.
UMPIRE, UMPIRE, WE NEED AN UMPIRE.

CH 9.
KILL THE BASTARD.

CH 10.
A LEAP OF FAITH.

CH 11.
WE COME IN PEACE.

CH 12.
A HOLY FATHER SINS.

CH 13.
CRAZY, I'M CRAZY FOR BEING SO BLUE.

CH 14.
STICKS AND STONES BREAK BONES.

HARMONY.

Concord or agreement in facts, opinions, manners, interests, etc., good Correspondence; peace and friendship; as, good citizens live in Harmony.

INTRODUCTION.

In honor of its Protestant Fathers, for only the second time in Harmony's one-hundred-year history, the town was fixing to celebrate Founders Day.

Her apple trees were ripe for the picking and so was every hidden secret amongst its residents.

After years of living in a township small enough to know about the forbidden subjects shoved deep into the darkened recesses of everyone's closet, the hatred that had begun to brew was deadlier than a pit full of venomous snakes.

But, just like Harmony, Nora Beth Toliver also had a secret.

Since her bitch of a mother finally died and being the only surviving Toliver and member of Nana's Kissing Apples Gang, she no longer had a reason to stay out of Harmony.

Just like Founders Day, it has also been over a hundred years since an ancestor of her family stood upon Harmony's hallowed grounds.

Her Great, Great Grandfather, Pastor Jonathon Tucker, had committed murderous acts and unforgivable sins before taking his own life.

To keep this secret hidden from the outside world, and so they would never have to be reminded of it again, the township sent his wife and daughter away.

Like every other caught sinner in the church, they were now outcasts.

If those who continued to reside here had to take matters into their own hands, they would have killed them on the spot that day.

Instead, the Tuckers, with the threat of death, were to never return for a visit or speak of what had taken place here.

Whether they liked it or not, Harmony was and would never be their home again, and that was just the way it was going to be.

But, Ms. Toliver didn't care.

Nora was either going to die all alone on the family's farm or next to Jonathon Tucker, the only Father she has ever known.

Hell, if they didn't watch it, Nora would gladly take a few of them with her when and if they tried.

Toliver Women, to this day, still carried the razor-sharp claw that Father Jonathon Tucker, just to save his very life, had defensively ripped from an eagle's leg.

Maybe, if she offered them a nice slice of pie that was so juicy it flowed like the sweetest comb of honey across an experienced tongue and shared the rich cider that dripped from her freshly plucked and squeezed apples, they just might let Nora stay.

Nora Beth Toliver!

Yes, Little Ms. Bitch?

Are you moving to Harmony?

Yes, Little Ms. Bitch.

Dumb-Ass Whore!

Just like your fucking Nana.

CH 1.
WHEN THE APPLE IS RIPE.

At first, Mark really didn't quite understand what he was hearing.

Somewhere within the warm breeze was a summer melody that has invaded his ears on more than one occasion. It's a buzzing sound or maybe an extremely high-pitched scream.

Something like that of a rage filled child which tends to go away within a few seconds after their angered father's hands grasp tightly around their little throats so as to shut their incessive tantrum the hell up.

He has always heard it.

As a kid, Mark liked to stop and listen to the insectoid symposium.

At times, he would focus with as much spirituality a child of his age could possibly muster or understand, and maybe, just maybe, Mark would hear a voice?

The universe would somehow share its unfathomable hidden secrets and let him know that he, she, or it, was aware of Marks feeble existence and this gay, ridiculously feminine little boy was not alone in this scary, fucking world.

Thus, saith God?

Thus, Saith God.

And then there was that wonderfully other lyrical chorus.

Mark has and will always be a sucker for those extravagant and quite expensive windchimes one tends to only find in those rich, snobby type of neighborhoods.

The swishy man's extensive collection wraps the entire three-hundred and sixty degrees of his Victorian masterpiece.

There had to be at least twenty or more just along the front porch alone.

Just make sure to watch your step when visiting, Dudley DoWright, "as he always does," would say. Mark seems to have an issue with a growing wet spot on the side facing his neighbor's house.

That's where the extremely hot Brawny-man lives.

It was such a bargain, to this day he still has a hard time fathoming why no one got to the bank before he and his partner did.

The chimes sounds were always such a soothing end of the day finish for Mark.

After work, he loved to stretch out on his favorite lounge chair underneath them and daydream about screwing around with the Grizzly Bear next door.

The young gay man loved to lay there smoking a fat ass joint, have a mixed drink strong enough that just a thimble full would kill a newborn child, and play with rocky who was always at full attention while drooling over the half-nude Stallion next door.

It seemed that today's chores would include cleaning the family gutters.

WOOF!

WHAT.

A.

VIEW.

That firm ass of Mr. check me out went on for days while the steeds bulge seemed to be quite large.

A decently sized package that was purposedly being shown off just for his neighbor's sexual pleasure or he was unintentionally sporting a semi hard-on.

Either way, who could ask for anything more?

He wasn't sure if it was his porch, the harmonious breeze, or possibly the hot pocket across the yard who had now begun to mow their lawn which caused Rocky to blast away.

The first of many pay loads to cum.

Every man, and woman, knows that rock hard feeling.

That welcomed, but unwelcomed poking and prodding for morning sex.

Mark was absolutely sure that if Mr. Parker ever demanded for him to bend over because he needed a piece of ass, all he had to do was yell.

I.

AM.

DADDY.

NOW BEND THE FUCK OVER!

Originally, when Mark and his Tom had first looked this place over, he had such dreams of eternal bliss living with his soulmate until death do they part.

As they worked together on the gospel of tolerance that so far seemed to be going their way, Mr. Padden would drone on and on about his fantasy of them growing old together while making a positive impact on Harmony's Protestant community.

He envisioned them walking the town hand in hand, while staring dreamily into each other's eyes.

Planting spring flowers and vegetables out in the yard.

Their hard, sweating, and often shirtless bodies glistening in the sun for all to see while Tom lovingly reaches over and brushes a speck of dirt from his sweethearts face.

And, as the wrinkles and time began to overtake them, he could still visualize them sitting together on that big ass porch wearing only their jockstraps during those hot summer nights.

Sipping homemade lemonade, whose recipe Mark had stolen from Toms mom, while watching an evening heat storm.

Or, seeing just how turned on they could get before slipping into a darkened part of the yard and exploring each other's rock-hard manhood's with every orifice available.

OHHHHHHH.

MMMMMM.

SLURPPPPPP.

Mark was so full of love and admiration for his partner, just the thought of them spending eternity together caused his overflowing pride to almost burst through the rib-caged walls of his puffed-up chest.

Especially when Mary, who just happened to be outside that day, shouted out from across her yard on how much of a dashing couple they made when she last saw them out enjoying their evening walk around Harmony.

Oh, the paganism of it all.

But, Marks Tom was a man's man.

There never will be any kind of an outward expression of their love when they were amongst the populace.

However, Tom would constantly assure Mark that he was every bit of a gay man through and through.

And once their bedroom door shuts, he will think that the devil himself showed up to ravage every inch of Mr. Padden's lustful flesh.

Other than that, no one was to be told they were lovers.

Ever!

Roommates, yes.

Family, or a long-lost cousin, no problem.

But, other than those who were already in the loop; to any outsider, Tom was nothing more than a straight man sharing a house with another straight man.

PERIOD!

As the O.G. Kush pulled him deeper into fantasy land, Mark, while daydreaming of his future Daddy, began to feel his nude and sweaty body meld into the new Adirondack furniture purchased just days ago.

When it came to exploring his manhood with long sensual strokes; the six-foot hedge which wrapped around that entire porch, gave him all the privacy needed.

And once Mr. Parker noticed Mark, it usually took just a matter of minutes after running his girls back inside their house, before Mary's Tom spent the rest of his day working on their personal lawn in attire that could almost be considered his birthday suit.

Shirtless, commando as usual, and wearing Mr. Padden's favorite pair of britches. Blue-jean cutoffs that were extremely short, ragged as all getup, and holier than a block of swish cheese.

Their peek-a-boo quality left nothing to the imagination of what may be hidden underneath its exposing intentions.

Harmony's extremely muscular stud, whose name just happened to be Tom also, was always semi-nude and sporting a package large enough to make out from almost any distance.

The best medicine ever prescribed to heal a crushed heart from a shattered relationship is to realize that the hairiest man in town was not only your neighbor, but the hunk seemed to be into public displays of voyeurism also.

Why else would he constantly dress so provocatively tempting?

But thanks be to the God's above that he was.

Mark finally believed that his demolished heart was going to heal much quicker than he first thought.

Have you ever noticed your neighbor's facial expressions when they think you're not looking or paying attention to their response concerning something you shared with them?

Especially after they see how you frivolously spent the excess money that fate had randomly tossed your way?

It begins with a quaint smile and nod of good for you, while wishing they had your stuff and you had a forty-four-magnum bullet hole in your head.

To make their relationship go away, without outing him to his now married wife, that's how much it cost Mark's Tom.

PRICK!

AND.

I.

DO.

MEAN.

PRICK.

GIRLFREIND!

BANG!

BANG!!

BANG!!!

Tom might have looked and acted like a Man's Man, but when Mark licked his sweet spot, that girl could squeal like a bitch in heat.

While they were having sex, the Alpha just loved to be planted on his back. Mark would spread his legs so wide that he looked like a Thanksgiving wishbone waiting to be pulled apart.

Kind of like those not so happy festivities most of us are dragged kicking and screaming too.

Except, this celebratory gathering comes with fireworks.

With his ankles tied to the chains back above his head, and completely helpless to every whim and desire his lover had planned for that day, Tom's response was always the same.

Once Mark shoved his unshaved face between the submissive's two hairy cheeks, sliding his tongue deep into that sweet spot where the honey is kept, Tom would begin to squeal like the true sex addicted pig he was.

As Mark, with Rocky in hand, was being carried away on an elixir of spirits; hundreds of extravagant wind chimes and their melody of relaxation and tone were sweeping him deeper into the sexual fantasy that was now possessing and cannibalizing every inch of his hardened and sweaty flesh.

Mark's very last thought, before passing out, was what a way to go!

Tom Parker was outside watching Mark closely that day too.

With his mounting headache, because of the cicadas and the approaching storm's atmospheric changes, he knew Mark and those damned wind chimes were about to receive the wrath of his anger.

If the fag did not secure them, as was requested by the town council, Tom threatened to close down Harmony's one and only Cider Mill.

And, if they did not agree with Mr. Parker and give in to his demands, he would do it on Founders day.

As the thunder and lightning began to explode over their township, hoping it would help to squelch the noisy insects, Mr. Parker pondered using perforated pieces of Mark Padden's pleading heart to plummily plug his portly plump ears.

Deep in the depths of a human's ear is a small vibrating bone which allows us to hear certain audible, and sometimes inaudible sounds.

There are many which we immediately recognize, and others we can only detect unconsciously.

So, as the siren's song began to scream its musical and intoxicating sound across Toms fluid filled eardrums that are located next to the brains blood and nerve highway, every last atom of Mr. Parker's flesh began to resonate in acoustical perfection.

As the physical sensations overpowered his mind, body, and soul, the top of his head, right down to the tip of his toes, began to tingle as if he was about to bust the biggest nut ever.

And so it was.

The overpowering vibratory sensations made Tom's bull sized nuts pulse and caused his thick, semi hard cock to shoot its musically induced load down his right leg.

During the townships first Founder's Day, there were a few survivors after the terror had ended that time the cicadas visited Harmony over one-hundred years ago.

And, as the last of those demonic insects finished scratching and crawling their way back into the burrows of Hell, the remaining congregants of The Blessed Flock began to slowly gather at the door of their polluted sanctuary.

They tried their best not to surrender to the tsunami of tears that was now threatening to drown them in a flood of shock, horror, and grief, but most, if not all, were quickly overwhelmed.

Before shuffling off to their homes, the conspirators unanimously agreed to cover up and never speak of the misdeeds that had been purposedly perpetrated by their Founders ever again.

And, after running the Tuckers off, those who survived the nightmare swore to stay and make sure their guarded secrets remained dead and buried with the Fathers.

But, to their future detriment, Harmony's Cicada's never agreed to the Protestant's dead and buried policy.

Once pregnant, it can take up to ten days before a female cicada lays her eggs. And, since they are born and go into heat at different times, the last male will not die until he has mated.

Neither, will its cries.

At first, Tom was glad to see that someone had finally bought the Henderson house.

Since Pastor Henderson went nuts and hung himself, his newborn son, and the rest of his entire family in the home's attic space, the structure has vacantly sat there for over fifteen years now.

Before his son was born, their all-girl efforts eventually reached the point that his family could actually form their own baseball team.

HMMMMM?

So, that's how many women it takes before a holy man goes mad.

Tom silently pondered what life altering catalyst to his psyche could cause him, in such a manner, to officially go nuts. Because, if they ever do have a son, it would be some great information to pass onto his own.

CH 2.
FABUOUSLY DELICIOUSE.

Like Mr. Henderson, Tom has always been a man of faith.

As a child, Mr. Parker's fanatical beliefs were strong enough that his overbearing mother often feared he would turn out to be some sort of a religious cult leader.

Nut cases who teach a warped sense of truth to anyone who is willing to listen, believe, and surrender their own free will.

All of whom get falsely indoctrinated while the false prophet, according to the word of God, fulfills his every want, whim, and desire.

So here, now living within his sight, was the first gay man Mr. Parker has ever, "knowingly," met.

One who would share his homosexual experiences with anyone who was willing to lend him their ear.

Shamelessly out and proud about any and everything an ungodly man could possibly endure or dish out concerning his alternate lifestyle.

The son of a bitch didn't even care if you thought the subject matter being discussed was appropriate or not.

Especially around children.

Just to have an open ear, Mark would continually spill his own dirty little secrets.

Every.

Last.

Fucking.

One.

When Mark was on his porch, showing off those rock-hard abs, Mary and the girls were never allowed to play, or work out in their front yard.

The way Mr. Padden looked at it, you needed honey to catch a bear and Mr. Parker definitely looked as if he liked honey.

If, by some chance he didn't like dipping into Mark's kind of honey pot, then that fug-ugly Postman Dudley DoWright, "as he always does," would have to suffice.

He tried hitting on Lieutenant Bishop once.

A mistake that almost cost him another nose job.

No sooner than Tom would step back out into the yard; Mark, with just his head showing, could be found chilling behind the hedges on one of those very expensive lounge chairs.

Mr. Parker hated the way he always made sure to let everyone know just how much each piece had cost him.

According to the town gossips, no one gave a dam.

There repeatedly seemed to be at least one unlucky person who just happened to be passing by, that would get caught by Mark and would have to listen to his whiny conversations of why did his Tom leave.

Why did his Thomas hate to be ousted as a gay man so much?

Oh, and by the way, guess how much I paid for that?

For some reason, only being able to see Mark's head above the hedge lined porch tended to creep Tom Parker out.

The cock sucker always seemed to be busy doing something, but Tom was never quite sure what it could possibly be.

It appeared as if his hands were tied up and working feverishly with whatever he had to busy himself with that day.

Probably another damned wind banger!

It can be quite amazing to see how many ways an item can be created and produced for the masses.

With the obnoxious number of gawdy windchimes encircling that beautifully restored Victorian era house, the loud clanging was quite deafening at times.

And even though Mark has only been here for a few scandalous months, his homosexual antics have already managed to cause quite a stir amongst the township.

Mr. Padden has received a substantial number of complaints from the Local Yokels, "as he liked to call them," to please secure at least ninety percent of the clankers during bad weather or they would force him to take down the chimes if he continued to willfully snub his nose at their ridiculous laws concerning excessive noise.

Policies that were suspiciously drafted only hours after he, "and you know who," hung up his entire arsenal of screechers.

Laws Tom was planning to enforce before that next summer's storm had a chance to pummel the town with its fury.

Mr. Brawny was just waiting to see what it was going to take before he gets so pissed off that he finally decides to say fuck it and act on his own.

And whatever decision he chooses to go with, better happen quickly because the skies of Harmony were beginning to darken and become heavily ladened with rain once more.

There was no possible way the township's waterlogged grounds could handle another round of drenching rains.

A sentiment Tom Parker agreed with when it came to Mark's fucking windchimes.

He was done drowning in their obnoxious lyricality.

Now, if he could only figure out a way to shut up the tree screechers.

While a fully nude Mark laid stretched out and chilling behind the beautifully trimmed hedge line that hides Rocky, the porch, and his personal business, Tom's seething anger started to boil.

Like the now raging storm that was about to burst upon the towns unsuspecting residents, He was ready to do some unnecessary destruction upon his unwary neighbor.

And just as the tempests and its high-powered downdrafts began to blast across Harmony, the melodies chorus of the windchimes from Marks massive collection began to be coaxed from the different materials from which the songbirds had been constructed.

The new blast of air sent a deafening acoustical wave of teeth grinding vexation racing across the lawn and adding to Tom Parkers confrontational rage.

That morning it started out as a slightly obnoxious ringing in his ears. But, by the afternoon, the noisome chorus had morphed into an overpowering buzz of symphonic absurdity.

It felt as if the blade of a skill saw was slowly ripping his brain in half.

The noise in his head seemed to ebb and flow into every individual thought, nerve ending, and extremity possible.

Tom Parker was slowly going insane.

If Mark did not secure those dam chimes before this next storm hits; Tom knew, like the undiscovered expanding aneurism in his brain, that he was about to blow his top and god help anyone who stood in his way.

So, as that nagging rhythm from his neighbor's wind-organs began to clang upon the cyclonic breezes which now aided in the cooing off of another hot summers day, Tom swore a blood vessel must have exploded in his head because of the blinding anger that now seemed to be shoved like a red-hot poker deep into his right eye.

Not even the gale-force winds that were about to pound the crap out of Harmony stood a snowballs chance in hell of cooling off the killing ambitions that Tom currently had for his gay neighbor.

A Mr. Mark!

Fucking!

Padden!

Hell, since most of his surrounding neighbors were already pissed, and it was only a matter of time before someone snapped, who would blame him for taking out Mark and his clangor-bangers.

So, when the cicadas continued to emerged from their slumbering sleep, Tom Parker, in a blazing fit of rage, went next door with hedge sheers in hand and planned to confront Mark about his refusal to obey the law once more.

If he had to, Tom was going to sever every single string and wire that was being used to secure the unnecessary garden accessory to that picturesque Victorian house.

Instead, the shocked onlooker got to personally meet Mark's friend Rocky.

For the first and last time, Mr. Parker got to see what a sexually frustrated homosexual actually does when they feel the need to blow off some steam.

While lost in his world of sexual exploitations, Mark wasn't quite sure which sound invaded his erotic daydream first.

The unexpected noise caused him to realize that someone was possibly on the porch with him.

He wasn't sure if it was how a large number of boards seemed to creek, like a footstep was in mid stride, or the muffled scream of shock and horror, which sent shivers of ice-cold death down his spine.

Kind of like that time, just after turning sixteen, his mother unexpectedly returned home early and had barged into his bedroom unannounced.

The shocked child-bearer found him tied up, gagged, and being gang raped.

That erotic experience was Mark the trough's first pig fest.

Thankfully, after she embarrassingly kicked him out of their religious household, there ended up being many, many more of these primal festivities.

So, with Rocky feverishly in hand and lost to the overpowering elixirs of lust and drugs; Mark, just as Rocky was about to blow his top, never noticed Tom storming across his lawn in a murderous outburst of rage.

Oh, what that Daddy could do to him.

NO.

QUESTIONS.

ASKED.

At first, it was hard enough to focus through the haze of pot and liquor, so he really had no comprehension of what was fixing to occur.

But, as he continued to fight off the hypnotic effects of the liquid and smokable party-favors, Mark shockingly realized that Tom Parker, the man he so lusted after, was now standing over him not just in a fit of hysteria from the windchimes, but pushed passed the brink of insanity from the sight of his gay neighbor laying on his front porch stroking his rock-hard cock.

The faggot was referring to Tom as Daddy.

He was also begging Mr. Parker to do things to him that the now shocked neighbor was sure only those screaming, unsaved souls in the tormented pits of Hell would hear.

1 COR 6:9

DO YOU NOT KNOW THAT THE WICKED WILL NOT INHERIT THE KINGDOM OF GOD?

DO NOT BE DECIEVED!

NEITHER THE SEXUAL IMMORAL!

NOR IDOLATORS!

NOR ADULTERERS!

NOR MALE PROSTITUTES!

NOR HOMOSEXUEL OFFENDORS!

Today, in Harmony, the buzz around town was the horrific murders of Mark Padden, by his neighbor of all things, and Tom Parkers entire Protestant family.

The happy couple has been married for over fifteen, unadulterated years.

And, at no time has anyone ever seen or heard the man raise a hand nor a strong word to Mary or the girls.

He was the perfect Husband and Father we all prayed and wished for as kids.

Mary was the most loving, faithful, and overly devoted wife a man could ever want or ask for. She was also the perfect wife and mother all good girls eventually hope to be.

Their girls, however, not so much.

As Mr. Padden's feeble life was being ripped from God's green earth, the blood curdling screams of a dying man's last breath was heard around two fifteen that afternoon.

Marks lifeless and severely battered body was found about an hour later by his mail carrier Dudley, "as he always does," DoWright.

The shocked delivery man found Mr. Padden just a few minutes before the muffled gun blast went off.

Dudley had been mindlessly delivering mail for close to twenty-five years and was finally about to retire.

He only had three days left.

This was not how Mark's future Daddy wanted to remember his twinkie little man-boy.

Since there would never be another knock on the door opportunity to gently kiss, touch, fondle, and stroke the lifeless boy's hairless and rock-hard body, Dudley DoWright, "as he always does," made sure to take his own sweet time.

Because, once the local yokel cops showed up, Mark would have been tagged and bagged, and Dudley would never have another chance to see how his massive cock felt inside the boy's still warm manhole.

DoWright's Daddy always said that you have to take it where you can get it, and that's exactly what Dudley did after dropping his trousers and tossing Mark's lifeless legs over his shoulders.

When Harmony's police force was finally notified, Lieutenant John was the first to show up.

And once Officer Bishop made sure to secure the scene; he firmly instructed Dudley not to touch anything before telling the out of breath mail carrier to zip up his pants and continue to stick around until Chief Bob gets here.

This way, he could canvas the area and see if any of Marks shell shocked neighbors could help locate where the shotgun blast had originated and not have to worry about someone else defiling the body.

Before the Army Corps of engineers carved out their canyon pass, Harmony was a quaint little town tucked on a ridge behind what used to be a death-defying trek up and over a severely steep mountain peak.

When it came to a tumble or misplaced footstep, there were no second chances before the road was built.

Back in the day, if you just so happened to fall while trying to access the remote town, it was pretty much a death sentence. That's one of the reasons why the United States Government demanded an access road be built.

So no one else would die.

To this day, most of Harmony's residents wished they had never agreed to the massive water trough. But, because they wanted to have access to the country's mailing system, the powers-that-be gave the small town no other option.

If Harmony wanted a post office, the USPS wanted a road.

It was a tit for a tat concession.

And now, because of their valley and that canyon road, the gun shots misconceiving echoes made it pretty much impossible to pin down its point of origin.

The last crime to be punished here was when a pimple faced group of teenage boys ran the towns new warning light.

Just in case anyone decided to drive over the cliffs edge, the blinking signal had been installed as a last-ditch safety measure so as to help protect the town from any unmerited lawsuits.

The dumb asses did it that very same day the flashing, three-way red light had been erected.

According to Chief Bob, after giving them all a severe ass chewing, three of them were sent home with the same threat he was administering to Tommy Dunn while shoving the violently resisting adolescent into the back seat of his patrol car.

I know your mom and pop.

Now get your butts out of here before I have to rim your asses!

An imposing threat that was always accompanied by a sinister grin and deadly laugh straight out of the Grim Reaper's playbook of make them sweat.

Between the bring it on glint in his eyes, that joker eat you alive grin, and the deliberate way Mr. Hatchet would run his wet tongue over salivating lips as if he was about to devour a prime rib, the young men quickly understood Mr. Policeman wasn't joking.

Tommy's chilling screams for them to run, also aided in their yes sir, no sir departure.

Because of the rumors insisting the town's head law enforcement official might actually be a sexual predator, no teenage male in his right mind was willing to chance Barney-Five's rim-job challenge.

But now, after eight long years, Harmony finally had another breaker of the law on its judgmental hands.

CH 3.
JOHN AND MARY SITTING IN A TREE.

With not a child or Mary in sight, John Bishop soon found the torn and ripped from its hinges front screen door of Mr. and Mrs. Parkers house tossed to the side of their porch and the blood-stained front entrance wide open.

No matter what, Mary and the kids were always home.

With two extremely rambunctious red headed little bees running around with a never-ending supply of atomic energy, it was just easier to send Tom out then having to bathe the rug-rats, dress the rug-rats, and finally get the rug-rats loaded in the car for whatever mundane errands that just so happened to be on her lists of honeydews.

One must always look presentably appropriate when out amongst the public.

Mary wouldn't have it any other way.

Because there always seemed to be at least one of the Hen House Chicks running around town, or behind a local counter with today's current gossip concerning Harmony's latest scandal, God knows you sure as Hell don't want those Bitches knowing anything about you and your private business.

Why?

Because nothing was safe or sacred once it has crossed the threshold of a Hens lips or ears.

WHAT!

SO!

EVER!

When it came to the Parkers, John secretly loved their two girls.

With the slightest hint of a hop, skip, or jump, they could send those bright, fire engine red locks of hair a bouncing.

It was mesmerizingly captivating how the suns shimmering rays danced across their heads. Hints of copper, bronze, and a slight whisper of strawberry blond exploded in the light.

They were only five and already lookers.

Maybe, it was the towns new light and not them which caused traffic to pause or stop in its tracks.

Whatever the cause, God help any boy or man who presented any idiotic thoughts of physically, emotionally, or mentally harming them, John Bishop swore.

Since the girls were his and Mary's dirty little secrets, he wasn't sure how to pull off that selfless act of a loving and devoted father without Tom Parker or Harmony's residents ever finding out.

Hopefully, without arousing any kind of suspicions from the unsuspecting man who is now raising his two kids, the overly devoting officer could just say, doing my civil duty Mr. Tom.

Just doing my duty.

While going from room to room, making sure to purposely investigate every closet, cubby hole, nook and cranny, including the basement, it painstakingly took John more than thirty minutes just to search the first and second floor of the blood-stained dwelling.

Anywhere a child or adult could possibly hide or be hidden, the startled investigator made sure to look.

Sometimes twice.

The last place the adulterer had to search would be up in the attic.

The stairs were hidden in the second floor's ceiling just outside his girls' pink and flowered bedrooms.

As a surprise for their fourth birthday, the strapping officer had been invited by Mary to help the Parkers paint. His enthusiastic response completely dumbfounded Tom that day.

The perplexed father just couldn't fathom why a single bachelor would spend his day off with a pink paintbrush in his hands instead of a hot and horny bitch.

That would have been Mr. Parkers first choice.

And now, John had another decision to make when it came to helping out the family. Should he continue the search by himself after just experiencing such a severe case of the heebie-jeebies.

Have you ever felt a shiver so cold your soul begins to scream out that something is not quite right with the world?

If so, you better watch your back.

Because you're either fixing to meet the Grim Reaper face to face; or, you are going to experience something that will haunt you and your nightmares for the rest of your life.

And those fears were not the only things John was experiencing.

He was also feeling an overpowering dread because his current situation could quite possibly be the last time he would ever see a morning sun rise so spectacular that one forgets to breathe.

That icy touch always seems to go from the base of his skull right down to the tail bone's tip.

Just thinking about his decaying and insect infested casket, with its licked clean whitewashed bones, finally destroyed any doubts he may have had about cremation.

If he really gave it some thought, no one really wants to spend an eternity with bugs crawling in and out of their ass.

Can you imagine the itch?

The other thing that was hindering the officer's resolve was when his heart seemed to stop after feeling the hand of death rake across his trembling soul.

No matter what crack or crevice it may be hidden in; every hair follicle, as if by magic, turns into millions of goosebumps.

Where in God's Hell did the term goosebumps come from anyway, John pondered.

As he imagined his soul feeding the hunger deep within the Reaper's cannibalistic bowels, the deputy couldn't help but to think that his demise would eventually produce a smile on Mr. Grim's bony and lipless face.

Seems that fiery pit of digestion can only be quenched with a reaping.

So, get ready Johnny Boy.

The death dealer has decided that it's time to harvest your pitiful waste of time and space life.

With a quicker than lightning swipe of his freshly sharpened sickle; Death, without a tear or afterthought, quickly reaps what's his before harvesting that next name on his damned list.

Hopefully, it's not yours.

NEXT!

WHO'S NEXT?

It was known that Mary had started her own little apple chip business up on the homes third floor. If it could be eaten, potpourris, or lathered, the entrepreneur made sure to cover all her bases.

The things Harmony's women could do with that fruit amazed John Bishop.

On more than one occasion, he was left completely speechless by their ingenuity.

Apple blossom soap was her specialty though.

John loved the recipe she used.

Her skin, without a soapy bitterness, tasted just like the flesh of Harmony's sweet apple's. He also loved how her cunt began to leak the sweetest apple cider the second his tongue touched it.

It was the best thing he has ever had the pleasure of nibbling on.

After that first taste many, many years ago, John instantly had two epiphanies.

Not only was he an addict for sweet tasting pussy; but, in his line of business, it was safer to label yourself a connoisseur instead of an addict.

That way, no one would second guess his choice of words about what he was actually doing with his spare time.

It was at this point, after he opened their trap door and started to pull down the attic ladder a shiny new apple proceeded to bounce down those fucking steps.

No sooner than the rogue fruit slammed into his mouth, John's split and bleeding lips began to instantaneously swell.

Kind of like what happened to Mary's honey pot after he spent over three hours at the all-you-can-eat buffet between her legs.

The excuse she had given to Tom for not wanting to be sexually active at that time was due to a yeast infection she had magickly contracted.

Mary blamed it on his uncircumcised cock and demanded that he scrub it better when taking a shower or get it surgically removed.

And, until that happened, sex was most definitely off the table.

As the lover stared blankly into the attic, John began to develop a very sickening feeling deep within his guts.

It's the kind of discomfort which makes someone think that they're about to crap their pants as the individual runs screaming for their porcelain god while trying not to shit themselves.

As the squirts begin to leak, even an Atheist will start to pray if the non-believer is one-hundred percent convinced they are actually going to crap themselves if he or she doesn't call out for some form of spiritual intervention.

Their religious conversion is spectacularly amazing.

John never could understand why the lavatory's goal line always felt as if it was purposely placed on the other side of a fucking football field.

For the first time in his short career as a law enforcement agent, Mr. Bishop was actually afraid.

Somewhere at the top of those long, drawn-out attic stairs, death, and nothing but death, was patiently waiting for his soon to be arrival.

And just like the lip splitting apple, the attics aroma suddenly came pouring down the stairs too.

He wasn't sure how someone could smell anything other than that overpowering fragrance of apples, but there it was.

A sweet, metallic odor.

It smelled as if her kitchen and the gun range had been combined into a very unique aroma.

And do to the perfumed fragrance of sweet apples, deciphering the two was almost impossible.

He really didn't want to go up there.

But, how could he not?

One way or the other, because of their infidelity, the day of confronting Tom Parker would eventually have happened.

John just hoped that He, Mary, and the girls, were gone before some fucking Hen, or Hens, clucked about their secret affair to Tom.

When John was thirteen, his mom had to go run some emergency errands and decided that he, for the first time, was old enough to be left alone.

And once that declaration of freedom was announced, the only thing the adolescent could think and focus on was what he planned to do the very second she pulled out of their driveway.

When the guys at school found out how he had never jacked off before, they spent the remainder of their day reminiscing, and excessively teasing him on how good it felt to strip down, kick back, grab your cock, and, until it explodes like a massive geyser, beat the meat.

Kind of like those spurting fountains found in Yellowstone national park.

Until Maxi found her fucking car keys, purse, and anything else women seem to need before heading down the road, John tried his best not to show just how giddy he was for this unchaperoned opportunity.

So, once she turned the corner and he felt it was finally safe to play, the hardening young man, with plenty of room to work, stripped off his clothes, cleared her kitchen table of all implements, and climbed on up.

For the very first time in his life, John kicked back and started to stroke his already hardening cock.

It was a massive job and would be requiring at least two hands these days.

Hands that were about to have some unexpected company.

Before realizing that she was out of sugar, Mary Parker didn't see John's mom head down their driveway.

She was too busy making Toms birthday cake.

Her and Maxi, "or Maxine to others," always shared and shared alike.

No one could have asked for a better best friend than these two women found in each other. Especially when it came to secrets, nosy bitches, and hard-headed men.

If either one needed something from the other, it was no problem to just pop in and help themselves to whatever ingredient or household product that was needed.

Even if the other was gone.

John never heard her footsteps or their back-screen door slam shut that first time.

Mary had literally come out of nowhere.

However, what did garner his full attention was the sharp intake of breath catching in her throat as she walked around the corner and found him spread eagle, head thrust back, and lost in his illusions of sexual gratification.

That public display of nudity and debauchery wasn't the actions that shocked Mrs. Parker as he continued to lay there while assuming the worst outcomes possible.

It was the pornographic words accompanying his fantasy.

The young Alpha Male was demanding that Mrs. Parker better do what she was told when it came to pleasing his every whim, desire, and fantasy.

NO!

QUESTIONS!

ASKED!

BITCH!

Not only did her unexpected appearance scare a pre-cum nut out of him, but his veiny, massively rock-hard dick began to instantly soften.

How was he going to explain this to his mother?

And why the hell was he doing such dastardly deeds on her freshly sanitized kitchen table nude as fuck!

This was where she made his favorite apple pies which would never taste the same again because of her son's lustful depravity.

Maxi also used this table to entertain the local Hen House.

The brooding flock's gossiping insight was a good way to inconspicuously keep an ear out on the town and help Chief Bob, unbeknownst to them, manipulatively run their town council influence off the rails.

John never had time to dwell on the fact that Mrs. Parker was not only standing over him now, because Mary had moved with such quickness, but she was also grasping onto his freshly diminished member.

At first, he was speechless.

But that hindrance instantly dissipated the moment she began to softly stroke it with those delicately sweet lips of hers.

The young Bishop was in complete ecstasy as his neighbor's rotating tongue licked and sucked his quickly hardening jolly green giant.

As his thirteen-inch cock slid past her adulterous lips, slamming into the back of Mrs. Parker's throat, the young man's muffled groans of pleasure suddenly exploded into an overflowing geyser of sweet cream.

Like every other horned up pubescent on the face of this planet, Johnny boy spent many nights dreaming about such an encounter.

He just never thought it would, or could, happen to him.

As the spirit of lust overtook her; Mary, in no time flat, ripped off her favorite sun dress, bra, and panties, exposing those beautifully tits and her recently trimmed heart shaped bush to him.

The young Parker just couldn't believe what he was seeing.

So far, it felt like a dream.

And that wet dream was about to get so much more intense.

John, as if he was in some sort of a drug-induced daze, perplexedly watched as a fully nude Mrs. Parker began to climb up onto the table with him.

While firmly grasping onto his dick, Mary forcibly drove her hot box in one hard plunge down every last inch of his horse sized member.

A thrilling ride that was not going to stop until she felt the stallion's pubic hairs at the base of his extremely long pole tickle the lips of her hungering vagina.

An indulgent excursion she has continued with Mr. Parker to this very day.

If only her other half could reach just half the places John did, they may have been able to pull their rocky marriage out of the gutter before it ever reached the hopeless state it was now dangerously teetering on.

But, even though her husband has around eight or nine inches to drill with, she knew her sweet spot was so much deeper than he was capable of reaching.

And now, for the first time ever, she has finally found someone who was equipped to handle the deep well drilling that was required when it came to tapping Mary Parker's gushing aquifer.

CH 4.
PLAY BALL.

To keep from instantly blowing his wad, John had considered focusing on baseball.

But, the rumors about Harmony's chief of police, "according to Tommy Dunn," steered him clear away from that fucked up game.

Instead, the young man tried his best to relive the times he would mow her front and back lawn.

Before their first encounter, just so he could quickly make some extra cash, Maxi's son had begged his mother to let him use their one and only lawn mower.

Really mom, John would guilt.

He was thirteen after all.

When it came to clothes, girls, and popularity, how else was he supposed to keep up with ever other snot nosed brat?

He needed to have a job, and he needed one right now.

So, after wearing his mom down and getting his way, Mary Parker ended up being her son's first paying customer.

And, to Maxi's wonderment, his only client.

When he first started to mow Mary's lawn, John would do his best too unintentionally peek inside her bedroom windows every chance he got.

Also, another one of his favorite things was to hug and brush up against her beautiful firm breast.

Particularly when she came outside to greet him in her insanely sheer halter top.

An accessory that left nothing to the imagination.

The other thing that rocked his world was to, "accidently," bounce his softball sized bulge against her hoochy-coochy while in their welcoming embrace.

She had the softest touch.

He also tried to focus on how she would bring out an ice-cold drink to cool him off with on a hot summers day.

Every single time, just to taunt him, Mary would slowly run a freshly squeezed glass of lemonade covered in those wet icy drops of dew, up along the back of his spine, across his chest, and down his rock-hard abs.

For some unknown reason, she always stopped at that first unbuttoned notch of his bulging jeans.

At a glance, she could easily tell that his cock was about to rip every stitch and seam of the straining fabric. The extremely worn garment was definitely passed its stretching point.

A light tug or pull and the pants would have easily shredded.

Had Mrs. Parker done this, she would have seen John's stirring anaconda within.

Just like the bitches in his school, maybe she was nothing more than a flirt and cock tease when they first started their friendly game of poke and prod.

A sentiment he no longer questioned.

Because John Bishop was about to find out his married neighbor was much, much more.

On that most glorious day of days, Mr. John not only got to beat his meat, but it was Mary, his mom's best friend, who took his virginity and finished him off with the most mind-blowing orgasm either of them had ever experienced.

And after their sexual encounter, when it came to showing off his massively growing Yule Log, the young stallion no longer had a problem with it.

******

Before Harmony's Hen House could come around that last bend in the race, Dudley, for the first time in his life, had the latest and freshest gossip.

Sweet Old Joe Beth, who works at the post office for just as long as he has, always seemed to know the latest occurrences taking place amongst the towns permanent residents.

She proclaimed it was her god given duty to make certain that it was also everyone else's fucking business too.

If you just happened to have personal information concerning the towns latest scandal and felt the need to tell someone, you had four choices to pick from.

You could use the telegraph, telephone, or teleJoe and Sue Beth Redd.

And wouldn't you know it, the Redd's were always faster.

Because the only known gay man in town had been savagely murdered, Dudley, since it was pretty much the end of his day, decided to stick around while John searched for suspects.

He was curious to see what Harmony's cop would find.

Dudley DoWright, "as he always does," was not ready to walk up on Mark and find one of the wind chime pipes plunged deep into his skull.

Seems one of the metallic tubes had been shoved into Mark's ripped out heart also.

It appeared as if he had possibly been stabbed in the chest first, because his blood was splattered anywhere it could reach.

This really sucks thought Dudley.

Ever since that first day he had come upon Mark nudely relaxing in a private section of his porch, Dudley had been tantalizingly drooling about raping the young man's sweet holes.

Just days before retiring, he had finally gathered up the courage to ask Mark if he needed an extra hand rubbing down that hairless body of his.

Because Dudley was so caught up in the possibilities of his fantasy encounter as he blindly approached Mr. Padden's front porch steps on this blustery day, the quietness of Mark's windchimes had unconsciously stopped the mail carrier dead in his tracks.

Thank God it did.

Otherwise, it would have been one of those loose pipes tossed out on Mark's front lawn that would have derailed him.

Mark's entire collection was strewn across his yard and that beautiful porch which wrapped around his entire house.

Except for the random few that still sported a string or two containing seashells, glass, or whatever material it had been produced in, all the other wind instruments appeared to have been cut or ripped from their support hooks.

Not a one was left in any condition, shape, fashion, or form from which it could create its beautifully orchestrated sound.

Dudley had almost tripped on one of the larger, three-inch pieces of pipe.

It would have surely twisted an ankle before sending him and the days sorted mail tumbling to the ground in a heap of distorted mess.

According to Mark, those monsters had cost him six hundred dollars apiece.

He would be dammed to Hell, as the queen so venomously put it, before giving in to the town councils dumb-ass ideals.

Tie them up.

Or take them down.

Those are your choices.

Chief Bob wouldn't even meet him half way when he offered to cut their numerous numbers in half.

It was their way or the highway.

REALLY!

Who does that Dudley?

Protestant cunts do.

That's who.

That was one of the last humorous observations Mr. Padden said to Dudley DoWright, "as he always does."

Mark's final declaration was the one Harmony's retiring mail carrier will always remember him by.

Those grouchy breeders who haven't had sex since their wedding day can just go and fuck themselves!

As he patiently waited, Dudley figured about thirty minutes or so had passed when those in the area heard a second scream pierce the air before another gun blast soon followed.

To Dudley, it sounded like some misbehaving kids were setting off some really old fireworks.

Or maybe, it could have been a backfiring muffler or even a stifled handgun.

He wasn't really sure.

While everyone tried to figure out where the screaming shot came from, DoWright, "as he always does," would say that for a brief second, celestial solitude fell across their town.

Sadly, before the mystery could be solved, within seconds the air was once again filled with the shrill cries coming from those damned cicadas.

The first of thousands to come crawling from beneath the hallowed grounds of Harmony.

Kind of like the Redds.

Those Hell bound bitches were sent here to torment anyone that was willing to listen to their gossiping games of guess who, what, when, where, and why.

Dudley has been working with Joe Beth Redd for over twenty years now and was one-hundred percent convinced the sisters have a personal relationship with Satan himself.

It wasn't until recently that her doctor's had finally diagnosed the crazy bitch with OCD.

Or Obsessive-Compulsive Disorder to those not in the know, she'd exclaim.

After so many years of working in the same post office, DoWright, "as he always does," was quite surprised that he hasn't gone completely bonkers just yet.

Joe Beth had so many ticks that on Dudley's best of days, he found himself bringing home only some of the crap she would do in a day.

Tapping her foot against the floor or backside of the front counter from where she was sitting.

TAP!

TAP!

TAP!

Her long, fake, Pepto-Bismol colored nails against the counters glass tabletop.

TAP!

TAP!

TAP!

Or, the one that causes Dudley's right eye to twitch so bad that it doesn't stop convulsing until after he falls asleep.

The metal end of Redd's eraser-less pencil against her now false teeth.

TAP!

TAP!

TAP!

TAP!

TAP!

TAP!

TAP!

TAP!

TAP!

Dudley didn't know which Tap drove him over the edge first.

The foot?

TAP!

TAP!

TAP!

The nails?

TAP!

TAP!

TAP!

Or the teeth?

TAP!

TAP!

TAP!

Maybe it was the new twitch he has just recently began to pick up himself.

TAP!

TAP!

TAP!

It usually takes Dudley a few minutes before he realizes were the tapping noise is coming from.

This time, it was caused by a fingernail against his own dammed teeth.

TAP!

TAP!

TAP!

If only someone would put a hole in that cursed skull of hers, she just might shut the hell up.

As Dudley stood there watching the Chief prepare Marks body for transport; he, with arms crossed and a finger in his mouth, began to stew over the bitches fucking O.C.D influence.

Since any and all complaints fell silently on their local postmaster's death ears, Dudley DoWright, "as he always does," was finally going to take matters into his own hands.

TAP!

TAP!

TAP!

Today.

TAP!

TAP!

TAP!

Would be the day.

TAP!

TAP!

TAP!

That infernal tapping.

TAP!

TAP!

TAP!

Was finally going to stop.

TAP!

TAP!

TAP!

CH 5.
APPLE SAUCE.

At one time or another, every man or woman involved in law enforcement has a moment of sheer terror sweep across them during their valiant career.

It will either happen when you are all alone and about to face the reason which has brought you to this point and time. Or, it could happen in front of those who are there securing the scene with you.

There is also the possibility that someone might just be video recording the day's events too.

As his flashlight began its sweep of their dimly lit attic, the first thing John perceived after climbing that last rung of the stairs were all the tables covered in apples, utensils, and dehydrators.

Mary used them to dry fruit, flowers, or whatever else she had plans for that day.

One side of their production room was set up like a kitchen.

Another area had been established for packaging and shipping the dried products to her many consumers.

The third area of the divided attic was the spot where her sweet-smelling apple blossom soap was mixed and batched.

Out of all her creations, that was Mary and Johns favorite product.

Especially when they were getting down and dirty.

Mary Parker not only taught John about sex; but, to this day, she has continued her special indoctrination.

She has instructed him on everything a real man needs to know when pleasurably treating a woman.

A real man, before he plows and plants the field, always pleases his seductress first.

A real man also knows were the erotic and orgasmic producing zones on a woman are located.

All of them.

And the last thing a real man does?

He never allows his female companion to finish the job without him.

Her shit is pounded until she passes out from an overwhelming rush of sexual bliss or cries uncle first.

Two body-numbing experiences Mary Beth is well versed in.

John Bishop makes dam sure of that.

Every single time.

When it comes to sexually arousing a woman into having an orgasm, God knows her husband Tom has no clue.

NOT!

ONE!

FUCKING!

BIT!

If it was not for John's manhood being almost twice the size of her husbands at the tender age of thirteen, Mary would have just slipped out of their house without the adolescent being any wiser to her unexpected presence.

Lustfully, Mrs. Parker couldn't shake off the thought of just how big it would finally be when he turned eighteen and quickly decided that she just couldn't wait until her neighbor's son reached the legal age of consent.

And that was when their forbidden relationship took off.

Whenever Mary came outside after their first sexual encounter, John, for the remainder of their first summer together, made sure to flirt every chance he got.

His favorite game was to, "accidently," brush up against her firm and supple tits.

And now, after all these years, she no longer had to wait for the lawn man's unintentional elbow brush. Instead, John went for more of a hands-on approach these days.

Because of his manual labor job back then, Mary loved how his young rough hands felt when he would squeeze, pinch, and pull on her firm breast and nipples.

John really missed those erotic cat and mouse games, but right now was not the time nor place to be reminiscing about days long ago.

People that shouldn't be missing, currently were.

And he really needed to find them.

Just off to the right side of Johns vision, that fourth work area appeared as if all the bushel baskets had been dumped on the floor.

Hundreds of apples were scattered any and everywhere they could roll.

Many appeared to have been crushed and stepped on.

The apple's juice from the fruit had started mixing with what appeared to be copious amounts of blood.

There was also a faint smell of gun powder within the aroma of her freshly made soaps.

Before she and John would get lost in their sexually erotic sessions, the adulteress made sure to rub this product over every last inch of her body.

Mary loved how its intoxicating scent made Mr. Bishop so starvingly hungry that he would, inside and out, devour every last inch of her using his extremely large fingers, overly long tongue, and record-breaking cock.

And now, because of Ms. Parker and their children, Mr. Policeman would end up following through with his end-of-life plans.

An event he never thought would happen to him.

Sadly, today we lay to rest another brother of law enforcement who met his demise as another statistic of suicide.

We'll miss you Officer John Bishop.

May you rest in peace.

Hoping against all odds that his intuition was wrong; John wasn't quite prepared for what he was about to experience.

Yet, here he was.

Except for Tom, their entire family was suspended just feet above the strewn apple covered floor.

Somewhere deep within his heart, mind, body, and soul, John's spirit screamed in horror for he now had to accept this undisputable fact of were his family was hanging out.

There was such a gentle, almost calming sway to them.

It reminded him of the chimes over at Marks place.

When the wind would blow, no matter how lightly, they would all seem to dance and sing so easily.

The Parker's, however, did not have that soothing song or rhythm Mr. Padden's would make.

These human wind chimes came with a sickening creak.

And, for some unknown reason, they seemed to blend perfectly with the noise from those infernal cicadas.

As his fear gave way to shock, Johns blood pressure began to rise.

The flooding emotions that began to overtake him were accompanied by a deafening roar. An earsplitting cry which seemed to be getting louder, and louder, and louder.

To Lieutenant Bishop, time seemed to almost stop.

It felt as if he had just spent an eternity in the screaming pits of hell.

The demonic shouts may have only lasted for a few seconds, but that was enough for him.

Hell was not the place he wanted to be right now.

That judgment would have to come at a later date.

But, as he tried to calm down; Mr. Bishop suddenly realized that the overpowering shrieks of chaotic terror and utter disbelief were coming from him and not the gates of Hell.

Mary and his girls had been hanged from the attic rafters.

Not only were their hands bound to the hangman's noose, apples had been shoved in the mouths of his two angelic and completely innocent little girls.

Tom had done this so their fighting screams of Daddy please don't hurt us, would be muffled and not overheard by the neighbors as they were hung by their loving and unconditionally devoted Father.

And when it came to Mary, a freshly made bar of apple blossom soap had been shoved in the mother's mouth.

As for Tom Parker, his scattered remains were laying at the feet of Maxine and Sally Beth.

He had used a shotgun to blow his head off with.

Except for the man's ears, everything from his nose up was gone.

As the distraught and spurred husband pulled the triggers, after placing the double-barrel shotgun to his face, He also, to muffle his own tortured screams, had bitten down on an apple.

DAM!

Right between the eyes.

The man really knew how to make an exit.

He even left a few comments before departing stage left.

Scribbled in blood and apple juice under his swaying family were these chilling words.

THEY ARE NOT MINE!

AND NOW THEY ARE NOT JOHNS EITHER!

He knew?

How?

John and Mary had done everything possible not to get caught screwing around behind Toms back.

As he took what would be his last breath of air, John accepted the only way he was going to stop the infernal ringing and ear assaulting screams from the Cicadas, and especially those that where escaping from the depth of his own soul, was to place the hand guns barrel in his mouth and without giving it a second thought, pull the trigger.

As an officer of the law, how else was he going to explain why such an emotional outburst had caused him to piss his pants?

Earlier that day, Mary had promised to leave Tom and bring the girls to be with him.

Now, there was only one way that was going to happen.

If John wanted to still be a family, He had to go and be with them.

And so he did.

A sacrificial event which quickly caught the Postman's undivided attention still at Mark's place.

Not only had Dudley been the first to find Marks body, but he was also the first person to discover John, Tom, Mary, and their girls.

Too bad the only gay man still in town was now dead.

Dudley was just starting to enjoy Harmony's colorful scenery.

When it came time for him to deliver the days mail, Mark was always stark ass naked on the porch.

It was really nice seeing him lying there all tanned and toned while letting the obviously turned-on servant of the government visit and ogle for as long as he wished.

Since his Tom just got up and left him high and dry, Mr. Padden really missed being subdued in another man's arms.

The feel of a hard cock pounding his hungry ass while being accompanied by that wonderfully oiled down skin against skin feeling, always got his motor running.

An engine that was in danger of never being turned on again.

According to Mark's neighbors, there were no other gay men in the town of Harmony. So, if Dudley ever wished to play, Mark was pretty sure he wouldn't have a problem with that.

Dudley DoWright, "as he always does," may not have had Clark Gable's looks, but who does?

According to most of the male-on-male porn magazines he's illegally obtained throughout the years, when a queer is truly horned up, any man with a hard and decently sized cock will do in a pinch.

Especially since the invention of paper bags.

Now, when it came to other things concerning the town's only delivery man; for one reason or another, every person living in Harmony eventually notices that sometimes important deliveries tend to go missing from their mailbox.

Nothing really big or expensive.

Usually, it was nothing more than a billing notice, letter, or magazine. And, until it was actually missed or needed, no one seemed to pay much attention.

It was the postal service after all.

But, when it came to Harmony's skeletal residents, Dudley DoWright, "as he always does," knew the address to every closet. Dudley has been collecting little things from Harmony's residents for over twenty years now.

He even had a special room made up in his house for them.

Taped, stapled, glued, and pinned to his Man-Cave walls were magazines, pictures, videos, and everything else he has deemed important.

The moment he got home from work, Mr. Postman loved to strip off all his clothes and drool over what his neighbors were secretly into.

Especially after one of his special visits with Mark.

He did all of that, and more, while tugging and smacking at his snake like cock that was accompanied by a pair of bull sized nuts.

By the end of his day, they were just waiting to explode.

And so was everyone else in the town.

Harmony's natives talked as if this quaint Garden of Eden had been created as an escape from a condemned and evil world.

It's Protestant residents actually believed that they could raise their families here in peace.

According to their Pious Whiteology, Harmony is and will always be a loving and sinless town.

To Dudley DoWright, "as he always does," the township, according to their mail, was just asking for a Sodom and Gomorrah judgement from God.

And because of what their Founders did in the past, the backsliding Protestant postal carrier knew that the towns remaining residents have definitely earned the Karma effect.

Earlier that day, Dudley was so looking forward to Marks surprised reaction.

Mr. DoWright couldn't wait to see the shocked look on his face after he whipped out his monstrous schlong.

The record breaker was thicker than a can of shaving cream.

The porn magazines Dudley snagged for his vast collection of memorabilia at times, showed that the twink was into men whose cocks were extremely thick and horse like in length.

Dudley might not have been much to look at, but after he was finished binding, raping, and breeding such a willing and obedient boy, Mark wouldn't be able to sit down on that sore and overly stretched out ass for at least a week.

Maybe two.

Seems the homosexual was into some of the most extreme sex available to a participant who was willing and able to do what was asked and demanded from them while subdued in a leather-master's dungeon of sexual torment and pleasure.

Sadly, that experimental interaction between Dudley and Mr. Padden had to be cut short due to extenuating circumstances.

Especially after the screaming began.

Since there was now a possibility that Dudley could be caught committing a felonious act of necrophilia, he quickly zipped up his pants and began to follow the screaming sounds that echoed across the valley right before the single gunshot destroyed Tom Parker's attic window.

An explosive blast that also gave away the pennant man's location.

And after going inside and seeing what all the fuss was about, DoWright, "as he always does," was able to retrieve Johns pistol without anyone being the wiser.

The Lieutenant had used the still warm firearm to blow his brains out.

Before he stood any chance of ending up on a morgue's slab this day too, Dudley, before going back to the post office, decided that John's gun would look nice in his collection.

And when the Postal worker crouched down and wrapped his hand around its handle, the smell of gun powder, fresh blood, and brain matter, with the sweetest fragrance of apple blossom soap, overpowered his senses.

But it wasn't until after he saw the head of Johns dead cock peeking out from his hoochie coochy version of short shorts, that Dudley was suddenly surprised to feel his own cock growing into a semi hard-on.

He now understood why Mary considered it an aphrodisiac.

John's attire always reminded Dudley of those skimpy versions men wore back in the seventies.

They left nothing to the imagination.

What-so-ever.

God, he missed those sinful days.

No matter what your vises or sexual cravings were, anything and pretty much everything was on the smorgasbord of lustful choices.

And there were many options to choose from on this most glorious of days.

As Dudley played pocket pool while contemplating his forbidden choices, he suddenly took notice of the masterful work that had been achieved by all those involved in the liaison of adultery, lies, and death.

John's splattered brains blasted upon the attic's walls and floor, were still fresh and steaming.

Where they had slid down the antique homes interior facade, a most unusual mural had been created.

This was the kind of splatter painting only a stupid, rich prick could afford. It was pretty much a guarantee that every swank museum on God's green earth would have fought to the death for this unusual creation of artwork.

And then there was the other masterpiece scrawled across the floor.

It seemed that Tom had found out who actually fathered the twins. And, at some point of the day, he finally decided to personally confront his wife and the bastard's two bitches.

Tom Parker, after taking a moment to deal with Mary and John's dirty little secrets, was definitely going to make sure that Mr. Bishop got his up and comings too.

If he had any say so, John and Mary's fairytale romance would never be given the chance to experience that happy fucking ending!

He was personally going to see to that.

There was no way in hell the scorned husband was going to allow them to spend the rest of their conniving, ungodly, and deceitful lives living in a state of perpetual bliss.

Unbeknownst to her husband, Mary had already mapped out their escape.

It was their anniversary and the only time Tom would ever break down and have an alcoholic drink with her.

First, Mrs. Parker would acquire their best fermented apple cider and have him drink a bottle of his very own.

Second, she would start out by strip teasing Tom with his favorite lingerie.

He had lustfully purchased it for her on their wedding night.

Third, she would fill the bath water with her special apple blossom soap and then they would take turns erotically scrubbing and cleansing the others no-no spots.

And last, but not least, Mary was planning on spending that entire day giving Mr. Parker the best sex he has ever had.

By the time she was finished seducing him, his balls would be drained dryer than the aquifer that used to sit underneath the city of Las Vegas Nevada.

Thankfully, all it ever took was a Wham, Bam, Thank Ya Mam, and off to sleep he went.

If it had not been for that one and only position he boringly used during sex, if she could actually call it that, their marriage just might have survived.

This anniversary, Mrs. Parker was going to make sure that there wouldn't be a chance of him possibly waking up until that following morning.

She was going to make sure of that by getting Mr. Parker extremely intoxicated with liquor and a few sleeping pills.

After that, Mary and the girls were going to grab what they had secretly packed up earlier in the day, and quietly escape into the moonless night with her precious lover, and father of the girls, John.

Too bad those plans suddenly fell through.

Instead, here they hung.

Mary and John's dirty little skeletons were finally exposed for all of Harmony to see, by Mr. Parker himself.

If it wasn't for that dammed ringing in his ears, and the severe headache that always seems to accompany it, Dudley DoWright, "as he always does," would have been pissing his own pants right about then.

Damned Cicadas.

For some reason, the insects have been worse this year than they have ever been.

With this new, and currently unannounced information, it was finally time for Dudley to head back to the post office and share the latest gossip with Sue Beth Redd.

Just realizing that for the first time in his life, he had the newest, honey like gossip to drizzle over Joe Beth's loose ruby red lips, caused his now rock-hard cock to throb and drip with anticipation of what was about to occur.

He gleefully hoped her response would be an overly shocked one.

Everyone in Harmony would hear that Mary had finally decided to leave Tom for John.

How Tom killed Mark.

Then, after that rampage, he went home and before blowing his brains out, hung the entire Parker clan. That's how John Bishop found them before he decided to take his own life.

Dudley could only guess that he just couldn't live without Mary or his girls.

She was, "according to Johns own words," such a fine piece of ass.

Mr. DoWright, "as he always does," would tell how John and Mary, since he was thirteen, had not only been sleeping with each other, but the girls were his and not Toms.

Since that first illegal encounter of their torrid love affair, he has been tapping that shit on an everyday basis.

He loved how she could devour his stupendously behemoth schlong without any hesitations.

Especially when she demanded for him to forcibly drive every inch of his overly blessed loins deep into Mary's hot melting box.

He pretty much came every fucking time.

Dudley would also share that since the very first day he moved into town, Mark has been lustfully yearning for his neighbor Tom.

Mr. DoWright, "as he always does," was planning to also let it slip that when Mr. Parker was working outside, Mr. Padden would lay on his porch stroking and fingering himself every chance he got.

His one and only goal was to see how many nuts he could coax from Rocky before Mr. Tom went back inside.

And then, after relaying all the information to the clucking Sue, it would then be time to head back and nudely stretch out before the floor to ceiling wall of information that he so lovingly refers to as Harmony's wall of shame.

The collection of magazines, personal pictures, love letters, and everything else that could be used to blackmail another, has been whispering its temptress invitation to Dudley the moment he stepped out the door for work each morning.

A random schizophrenic occurrence that started many, many years ago and has now become an overwhelming voice that demands to be sexually pleasured on a daily basis.

His undivided attention was needed at home, so he really needed to hurry his ass up because, after screwing Mark and John, the necrophile's satyriasis cock was needing to blow off some steam once again.

Now, when it comes to things unseen, every postal carrier in the world sees and delivers obscene mail on a daily basis.

For over twenty years now, Dudley DoWright, "as he always does," has been secretly stealing, reading, and collecting Harmony's hellish secrets.

And for the first time in Dudley's dull and worthless life, people were finally going to look to him as Harmony's man of the hour.

That one person who was most aware of what was actually happening in town.

There has never been a time in his life were people have looked to him for anything other than the daily mail. However, once in a while, someone would give him an occasional Happy Holidays slap on the back before bitching about a missing bill or letter.

When it came to those specially cloaked books, toys, or magazines mailed in an inconspicuous brown paper wrapper, their arrival was always overly anticipated.

If it wasn't delivered by whatever celebratory occurrence they were planning, anniversaries, birthdays, and valentines being the main ones, horned up husbands, and especially wives, would lose their shit.

And the only reaction he usually got from their rotten and spoiled brats if something they were expecting unexpectedly arrived late, was to be punched, rocked, or mocked.

Dudley didn't know which was more offensive.

The fact that people actually saw you and just wanted to use you for target practice, their personal therapist, or a, "you didn't hear it from me," gossip transmitter.

The one that really got his goat was when they deliberately chose to ignore him, like he didn't exist at all, and push past their postal carrier as if he was some sort of plague victim or ghostly apparition that only the dead can see.

No wonder school kids these days snap and try to take out the ones who treated them like a useless, rotting bag of trash.

How else can a bullied child be expected to react after having to go through life wishing they were invisible, but at the same time seen?

CH 6.
DUDLEY, DUDLEY, DUDLEY.

When Dudley was born, his dad said that he was not only the smallest, but sickliest child the man had ever seen. And from the moment he was born, Dudley's father pretty much had nothing to do with him.

And he really hated his dad for that.

He also detested the force-fed institution of public education the sperm donor used to imprison him in.

From the very moment he started school, right up to the day he graduated, Dudley's teachers, the jocks, the dweebs, the geeks, and the nerds who shared the overcrowded hallways with him, always made sure to let Dudley DoWright, "as he always does," know that he was the weakest piece of pitiful shit in existence.

The only reason he was allowed to walk this earth was for theirs and Daddy's hateful pleasure.

Gym was the worst part of his day.

He had reached an age where showers were mandatorily expected and a vital part of their final grade.

Because of the prepubescent micro-cocks every last one of them seemed to sport, the other guys, out of pure jealousy, made his life a living hell.

Unlike them, Dudley would never have to identify himself as a grower and not a shower.

When soft, close to eight inches hung between his legs.

But when that monster was hard, it stood around twelve inches in length.

The baby arm sized girth didn't help either.

He was considered a freak amongst his classmates.

Sadly, at such a young and inexperienced age, Dudley had no idea that he had been truly blessed in the nether regions.

So, when it came to targeting him for punishment, rumor, and ridicule; his male classmates, in front of their entire school, would purposely strip every piece of clothing he had on.

Extremely large groups of girls where their favorite audience to amuse with their shock and aw escapades.

Maybe, that's why his dad was so jealous and why he seemed to abhor and despise Dudley's appearance.

Just seeing how your son's dick is way bigger than yours as he nudely walks out of the bathroom, would be enough to send any son of a bitch father into a frenzy.

How is one kid supposed to survive when you spend your every day, from sun-up to sun-down, feeling like a hunted and trapped animal by the man who, "supposedly," decided years ago that he would raise you as his own?

At which point in the relationship did he magically become the rotting animal corpse that had secretly scurried into his house before dying?

Now, after years of pretending to be his father, he could finally bury the young DoWright's emancipated body somewhere out in his back yard.

Dudley's Father continually joked about digging a hole under his beautifully award-winning roses, for which he is unmistakably known for, and placing his sons body there.

Screw that!

Even then, daddy would still have to smell your bloated carcass and have no other choice but to accept the undeniable fact that you still, and always will remain on his private property.

To Dudley, "in the eyes of most stepfathers," it's just better to either not marry the kids mother or run the rug-rats ass off before feeding that ungrateful little shit and pretend you never had to deal with another man's bastard.

Yes sir, that's why Dudley joined the United States Postal Service.

He quickly realized at an unmistakably early age that if an adult has or is trying to keep a secret, you could always find out what it is by reading their mail.

For years, Dudley had walked over two miles back and forth from his home to school and one day found that all the mailboxes along both sides of his street had been smashed to pieces.

Their valuable contents had been strewn across the road and lawns of his entire neighborhood.

Being the innocent youngster he was during that time; Dudley had no idea people could get such erotic material hand delivered to their private houses.

There was porn, clothes, food, and, according to the instructions, some really unusual items for which he assumed were to be used during sex.

The products used to stimulate a person's appetite in and out the bedroom blew his teenage mind and pocket rocket a little bit later that afternoon.

And after years of delivering, stealing, and collecting his so-called neighbors and pretentiously fake friends mail, Dudley pretty much knew every hidden secret that could be inconspicuously delivered inside a brown paper bag wrapping.

There was Mayor Adams, who had an extensive collection of illegal firearms.

When the world finally decides to take a fucking shit, he planned to use them on anyone and everyone who uninvitedly came through the front or rear door of his bug-out shelter.

Even if his own mother-in-law showed up, invited or not, and tried to beg or steal a drink of water from the well he had drilled in a hidden part of his basement, he'd shoot her fucking ass too.

The local preacher of Harmony's Protestant Church was secretly a polygamist.

At last count, Dudley thinks the preacher man was now up to wife number eight.

He had demanded that every single letter addressed to Daddy West was to be privately delivered to him in person by Dudley, "as he always does," DoWright.

Seems that when it comes to screwing round, why go online or hook up with the nights whores?

That's how one gets caught eating from the cookie jar.

Pastor West explained to Dudley one day that he had it all worked out.

The first thing you must do is leave your homeland.

The second thing you must do is to find a submissive and overly grateful wife in the third world country that you are currently doing the Lords work in.

That way, you can have the better of two worlds.

Church conference my ass!

When his wives' got too overly controlling or verbally uptight from his lack of nesting, Preacher West always, "and conveniently," had God's work to do.

Time to save the desert's nomadic children.

Those water wells aren't going to dig themselves.

Anna knew, (SMACK), that their estranged marriage was on the rocks.

It seemed that every time she tried to use scripture to point out that GODS first commandment was to be fruitful and multiply, (SMACK), and it got over heated, (SMACK), the man upstairs always seemed to call her pastoral husband away.

Maybe, that's why they, (SMACK), never had any children?

She would have turned out to be the mother from hell.

So, God and Pastor, (SMACK), decided it would be best to keep her fat, depressed, and utterly barren.

A revelation she was having a hard time dealing with, unlike her abusive husband.

The preacher's timid wife was all a dominate, (SMACK), and sadistically, (SMACK), controlling man could ever ask or dream for.

A passive, (SMACK), fat, (SMACK), low, (SMACK), self-esteemed gal who was, (SMACK), responsible for running the churches festivals and latest fund-raising schemes.

The selling of baked goods was their specialty.

Seems a working bee is a busy bee.

Buzz.

Buzz.

Buzz.

Just how he, (SMACK), liked to keep them.

Now, if he could just, (SMACK), figure out how to slap the sassiness out of her, (SMACK), without leaving any resemblance of a mark, (SMACK), they would all be hunky dory.

To keep her husband's righteous anger at an arm's length, (SMACK), Sara had decided that it was just best to occupying her thoughts and free time with other things.

Those quaint little tea parties sure helped her forget about having children.

For pretty much of their entire mind-numbing day, the women would sit and share Harmony's latest secrets while discussing which sinners needed to be saved first.

KLUCK.

KLUCK.

KLUCK.

By the rumors Harmony's Hen House was now sharing about her husband, Anna was absolutely certain her marriage was on the road to perdition.

So, to help quench the violent intuitions that seemed to overpower her husband, (SMACK), she had, (SMACK), decided to do whatever sexual acts her sadistically perverted Pastor demanded.

SMACK!

SMACK!

SMACK!

By willfully committing these vial acts, the First-Lady of their Protestant church dared to believe the wayward pastor would hopefully run back to her and not into the arms of another whore who in all probability, just to cover his tracks, ends up dead and buried down by the river or she becomes the coroner's latest jane doe who ends up in an unclaimed plot at some randomly picked cemetery.

Dear God in Heaven, let him be seeing another living and breathing woman and not a homosexual man she had so cried out to God while saying her prayers one day.

More like eight; Dudley DoWright, "as he always does," so blatantly put it, while dropping off their mail to her yesterday.

When it came to the post office, Mondays and Fridays were usually their busiest days.

The wanna be Alphas, never minding if it was a man or woman, were the worst.

This parcel better fucking be there first thing Monday morning or by the end of this fucking work week! If not, you were all dam well going to hear about it after their boss finished reaming the ass of your fucking boss.

NOW, WHERE'S MY PACKAGE BITCH?

Thankfully, with it being only Wednesday, the mail counter looked and ran as it always does.

Slower than a dead snail trying to drag itself across a forgotten section of Route Sixty-Six in the backwoods of rural Oklahoma.

A frivolous act that was going nowhere fast.

So, Joe Beth's day perked up nicely when Sue Beth enthusiastically strutted in for her daily round of gossip and mail.

It never fails, no sooner than Sue Beth entered those swinging glass doors with her favorite phrase, "Girlfriend, let me tell you what," Joe Beth had no doubt, what-so-ever, that it was going to be an extremely juicy conversation.

By the time Sue was finished dishing out on who, what, when, where, and why, Joe Beth was going to need a mop and bucket to soak up the massive amounts of drool caused by the juicy tidbits of freshly gleaned gossip.

The Beth's had become much closer sisters throughout their years.

Just like the Siamese twins Change and Eng, they had always dreamed of having that kind of connected at the hip relationship. Yet, for some unexplained reason, they seemed to have a lot more in common these days.

Other than talking about your neighbors, there really wasn't anything else to do in Harmony.

Their post office was promptly closed by four thirty.

Harmony's only bakery shut down at six.

While maxi's candle shop, because it was storm season, stayed open till seven.

That pretty much wrapped up any and all excitement.

For the rest of their evening, the Local Yokels would have to look for other hum-drum things to entertain them.

Years ago, because of that mindless boredom, Joe Beth had placed an ad in their local newspaper. She was wanting to start up an all-girl's book club.

Any mother who was bored with the never-ending chores of housework that seemed to magically multiply for all eternity, was invited.

Also, every woman who was tired of feeding those hateful, spoiled, always ungrateful rug-rats should give her a call too.

Even the single ladies of Harmony had been invited also.

For those who are married and tired of waiting on their lazy, dead-beat, good for nothing husbands to get off their fat asses and finally do something around the house, they should tell the son-of-a-bitch to just fuck off and come over for a spot of tea and biscuits.

They will be discussing the town, its future, and the latest bestselling book. That reading material had been suggested by her favorite daytime talk show queen.

Sue Beth, sisters to the end, was first to answer.

Sara and Amy Beth Windgood was hot on her heels.

Only God knows how they accomplished that feat.

It wasn't long after that first meeting, their town had officially named the noisome group the Hen House.

Seems if you ever wanted to share your personal business with the rest of Harmony, just let a Hen find out and everyone else would know every last succulent detail before the days end.

Like any good baseball player trying to steal home plate; Sue Beth, before picking up her mail, quickly slid up to the counter so she could tell Joe what had happened across town just as Dudley was entering the postal building from its rear entrance so that he could also let Joe Beth know what he had personally witnessed.

Before Mr. DoWright, "as he always does," could even cross the sorting room out into the front lobby where Joe Beth was wasting another day by not doing a dam thing, his ears perceived a tale of who shot who, who was found hanging in their attic, and who killed himself from the shock of it all.

Sue Beth was astonished that all of this had happened just down the street from her own front door.

If it was just about Redd beating him to the punch, Dudley DoWright, "as he always does," would have been okay. But, while Sue was telling her story, Joe unknowingly began tapping an overly excited foot against the tiled floor.

Due to Redd sitting in that same position for hours and days on end, its white printed design had been worn off long ago.

TAP!

TAP!

TAP!

John's gun that was hidden in Dudley's pants pocket was still slightly warm and oh so smooth.

TAP!

TAP!

TAP!

It seemed to fit perfectly into the palm of his hand.

TAP!

TAP!

TAP!

Like his cock, he wondered if its load would blow when he pulled on its trigger?

TAP!

TAP!

TAP!

Dudley DoWright, "as he always does," figured it was about time to figure that mystery out.

Without saying a word, the soon to be retired postal worker decided to end that infernal TAP, TAP, TAP, before it could possibly sink deeper into his own subconscious and, once again, find himself at home Tap, Tap, Tapping away.

With the girls so lost in their world of gossip, neither of them paid any attention to Dudley as he, with Mr. Bishops pistol, calmly walked up behind Joe Beth and raised his right hand to the back of her soon to be hollowed out head.

Since the massive headache began to rip through Dudley's brain, every physical and mental sensation within his body started to be overwhelmed with the deafening sounds of what can only be described as thousands, and thousands of cicadas.

Joe Beth Redd's demise took all the determination and focus he had.

TAP!

TAP!

TAP!

CLUCK!

CLUCK!

CLUCK!

BANG!

BANG!

BANG!

As if the creature from those alien movies was trying to take her out also; Sue Beth, right before her very eyes, watched the front of her best friend's face explode.

Dudley, while it was happening, found a sickening pleasure in her shocked expression of disbelief and horror.

The gleeful little chuckle that escaped from the Postal Carrier's blackened heart seemed to calm and soothe his tortured mind.

Sadly, the quietness lasted but for only a few seconds.

Sue always bragged that when her time came, for some unknown reason, she would get to see her own death. In a sickening sort of way, Ms. Redd seemed to find pleasure in it.

Just as she was sharing her news, Dudley came strolling around the corner.

It wasn't unusual for him to be carrying something up front for a customer.

As he walked up behind Joe, raising John's gun to the back of her head, Sue Beth really didn't pay much attention to what he had in his hand before a blinding flash erupted from between the two postal workers.

Sue Beth couldn't help but notice not only the look of bewilderment on Joe Beth's face, but how her deep blue eye's looked as if they were watching the bullet as it exited from just above the bridge of her nose.

Dudley's shot had exited right between her eyes, shattering Redd's horned rimmed glasses perfectly in half.

Seems their mom was right.

If you keep crossing your eyes, they will stick that way.

And that was all the time Sue Beth had.

Just enough to see her sister's final expression as Joe Beth's face distorted into what could only be called the best reaction to a horror movie ever filmed for the big screen.

An academy award performance if Sue Beth ever saw one, before the raging bullet passed from between Joe Beth's eyes and right into sweet Sue Beth's skull.

Sue had finally fallen in love with the thought of having Joe as a sister.

It was those dammed horn-rimmed glasses she continued to wear after high school.

When Joe Beth was around fifteen, just to tease and scare the other kids, she used to run around cross-eyed while also doing the same thing at home.

Redd loved tormenting their parents.

Her mother would constantly tell Joe that if she didn't stop, they were going to stick that way. So, one very cold and wet morning, Joe came into their kitchen screaming and crying.

She swore that she couldn't uncross her eyes and gave the Oscar winning performance of a lifetime.

Their mother, as she frantically searched for the car keys, was so convinced she had finally gone and done it, that Joe was immediately swept up and thrown into the family's vehicle.

When Mother Redd slammed that car into reverse, the force shoved Joe Beth out of her seat and onto the floorboards.

And after seeing her mom's shocked reaction, Joe was no longer able to keep up such an award-winning performance and began to hysterically laugh.

Well, you can imagine her response once it slowly began to dawn on Mrs. Redd how her lying daughter had pulled such a dirty little trick on her.

A flood wall of extreme boiling anger came over Mrs. Redd. And as she was about to beat the child into next week, their mother had one of her best brainstorms ever.

Ms. Joe begged her mom to spank her, punish her, anything but that.

Instead, her mother pulled out their great grandmothers old horned rimmed glasses from the dresser drawer next to her bed and placed them on Joe's face.

She instructed her prank pulling daughter that for the next few months she was going to wear them to school every single day.

From the second her alarm clock went off, until it was time for bedtime, they better be on her face.

No And's!

No If's!

No But's!

They were to be worn at all times.

So it was, on that first day back to school, Joe Beth Redd became known as Bat Girl.

After she showed up wearing them to her first morning class, it didn't even take her classmates but a second to blurt it out.

Look, Paul Spears shouted.

IT'S BAT GIRL!

Because Sue loved her sister so much, and didn't like Joe being picked on, Sue Beth, before their next day's classes, ran home and found their grandmothers spare pair.

And in support of her sister, she also wore them to school.

Seems the nickname Bat Girl didn't sound so bad to Joe once Sue Beth joined the team.

After all these years, standing behind the postal counter, Joe Beth was still wearing those exact same pair of horned rimmed spectacles.

The Bat Girl glasses that had haunted her throughout all of High School, were being blown in half by Dudley's screaming bullet.

The deadly projectile that was now heading Sue Beth's way.

Death's cold clammy hand entered through her right eye, shattering the bony structure behind it, and began to bounce from one side of Sue's Beth's brain to the other.

By the time it was done, her mental capacity had been turned into a liquid mass of jelly and ooze.

As their bodies crumbled to the tiled floor, in a kind of macabre puppetry, both women seemed to collapse in unison.

Even then, after it was all said, done, and over with, Dudley couldn't help but hum to himself one of his favorite childhood songs.

It came from that wonderful movie, The Wizard of Oz.

His Dad hated the Hollywood blockbuster so much that he, at the age of eight, was forbidden to watch it ever again.

It was for little children and he was just too damned old now.

Ding-dong the Redds are dead.

Which old Redds?

The gossipy Redds!

Ding-dong the gossipy Redds are dead.

They've gone were the bitches go.

Below! Below! Below!

Below! Below! Below!

Ding-dong the Redds are dead.

So, rub your eyes.

Get out of bed.

The gossipy Redds are dead!

Two Hens with one shot.

Harmony couldn't have asked for anything more.

Dudley loved that song so much and because his dad was such a dick, that he, while they were putting his ass into the ground, had even sung and danced to it on top of his own father's grave.

Thankfully, no one but Dudley and the gravediggers had been present.

While they stood there flabbergasted, Dudley DoWright, "as he always does," had no qualms about letting his dumb struck audience watch the Emmy winning performance.

As the towns postal carrier thought about all of Harmony's now dead residents, he just couldn't shake off that image of the Parkers quietly swinging from the rafters in their attic.

Except for Mary, Dudley pondered why Tom had put apples in the mouths of his family.

Just like the two coins needed to cross the river Styx, the postman began to wonder if the boatman also needed something to eat.

He might not have had two coins for his trip, but he did know where to get an apple.

With that revelation, the orchard down in their valley did seem like a nice place to go and hang out for a bit.

Since it was now past four thirty, Dudley DoWright, "as he always does," decided it was time to close up shop and give that new spool of rope he had ordered days ago from the hardware store, a try.

Since childhood, he has always wanted to have a tree swing.

But, because they could be dangerous, daddy dick never would let the bull in a China shop have something he could possibly hang himself with.

The boy was an accident just waiting to happen.

Today, however, that no you can't have a neck-breaker was going to change.

Dudley would see to that.

Harmony's giant tree down in their grove would make a perfect place for one.

So, even if it kills him, Dudley DoWright, "as he always does," was going to swing from its highest branch.

The retiring civil servant was pretty sure that if and when the girls were found, Harmony's residents could finally take that deep sigh of relief everyone was so desperately needing.

Almost half of the Hen House was now dead, and he was one hundred percent certain that no one would accuse him of doing it.

Why?

Because Dudley DoWright, "as he always does," was just a meek pip squeak and wouldn't hurt a fly.

Yes sir, they might have given a sigh of relief, but, with his own disappearance still remaining unanswered, it wouldn't last long.

All Hell was about to break loose.

Especially after they go looking for him over at his place.

And that's just what happened.

Before all of the towns private secrets could possibly be exposed, Chief Bob called Postmaster Don about his missing employee and the two dead sisters.

He also told him what they found inside Dudley's house.

And after hearing that, Mr. Garcia then called Tommy Dunn and sent his only remaining postal worker over to Mr. DoWright's, "as he always does, (but not this time)" to clean up the massive collection of stolen mail.

Every single resident, from the children to its adults, had something on that wall.

If you could send it, name it, or claim it, it was there.

From adult to child porn, adulteress letters, homosexual literature, bestiality pictures, snuff film memorabilia, and all manner of personal letters and bills were found tacked, stapled, or pasted to the homes interior walls.

Besides Dudley's sticky, red leather chair, no other furniture was found inside the four roomed structure.

That entire house had been turned into some sort of a sexually perverted alter.

What Don didn't share with the Chief, before they skipped town, was He, Pastor West, and Mayor Adams were leaving Harmony a week before Founders Day and would not be returning until after all of the mayhem has subsided.

They had unanimously agreed that these people were nuts and completely off their fucking rockers and wanted no part of their falsified festivities.

The three of them, "Hell, he might as well include Anna, it is her fishing hole after all," were not Local Yokels, "as they referred to Harmony's residents," and until it was all over with, they would not be stepping foot in this town again.

For the second time in its history, concerning whether or not Founders Day was actually happening, Harmony's residents had literally ripped each other to shreds.

There were so many back-alley deals made, either to achieve or stop this celebration, that each secret was drained for all its worth.

Kind of like when the screaming swine gets its throat slashed right before the luau so it's blood can be collected for their favorite soups and recipes.

Harmony's residents were even willing to compromised their sexual morality.

Seems that when it came to lewd favors, every last carnal pleasure had been traded for hidden secrets.

Nothing, what-so-ever, was off limits.

Fuck that!

These three men were taking Anna fishing.

The Pastors wife had expressed to her husband that she would do whatever he demanded.

SMACK!

SMACK!

SMACK!

If taking a sexually submissive role would somehow save their marriage, then Mrs. West was on board.

SMACK!

SMACK!

SMACK!

So, with Anna as their bait, they were headed out to Mayor Adams cabin for an entire week of fishing and exploration.

The three friends were going to properly instruct her on how to handle their hard and shiny poles.

SMACK!

SMACK!

SMACK!

In anticipation of the sexual free-for-all, they have been hand waxing those babies for over a week now.

The trio were also going to teach her that it was okay for guys to triple dip a marshy sluice at the same time.

SMACK!

SMACK!

SMACK!

Especially when the fishing was oh, so good.

SMACK!

SMACK!

SMACK!

That very first day, just hours after the foursome departed, the cicadas horrendous blood curling chorus began.

Not only were they looking for a mate, but they were also calling out to their earth mother.

And due to the reverberating insects mind-numbing screech, nine people were officially dead before the end of their first hatching day.

CH 7.
DON'T SIT UNDER THE APPLE TREE.

What used to be a sweet and quaint little town called Harmony had transformed into a den of pit vipers due to its secrets finally being exposed.

Seems that if the town's residents felt the least bit threatened, they would strike out at whoever gossiped first. Particularly if it pissed them off in any way, shape, fashion, or form.

As the sun began to set over this Norman Rockwell of a town, it's residence went home, locked their doors, and began contemplating their own hidden secrets.

They wondered who would come knock, knock, knocking on the front door, or who would maybe, "just maybe," snatch them up in a dark alley somewhere so they could privately take out their raging revenge on whichever poor soul that individual had a beef with.

When it came to the fights concerning Founders day, for those few residents who remained, their hearts were no longer in it to win it.

And neither was Mother Earth and her tormenting children.

To show her sorrow for what was about to happen, the tears of she who watches over us, began to rain down from above.

No one consciously noticed that because of the storms, the ringing in their ears being caused by the cicadas continuous screaming had quietly subsided.

Those brief moments, during those heavy gully washing down pours were a God send.

In the numbing days that followed; houses were shuttered, wakes were planned, the dead were buried. Their sins, along with Harmony's past, was once again stuffed into the farthest reaches of the town's hidden closet.

Harmony's surviving residents just didn't have time to dwell on the facts that some very serious and ugly secrets had been revealed by the now missing Dudley DoWright, "as he always does," and his infamous walls of shame.

That's because there was still so much work to do.

Chief Bob still had a festival to stop.

Don Garcia, the Postmaster, had decided right before skipping town, Dudley's soon to be empty postal rout needed filling.

So, he finally broke down and hired Tommy Dunn to stand in the void.

And for the first time ever, Tommy had been given the power to make all authoritative decisions concerning those things found in Dudley's spooged house of yuck while the boss and a few of his buddies went fishing at the most glorious hole he has ever encountered.

When he was a teenager, Tommy's mother had decided that a father figure was desperately needed to guide and make him into a man all parents hope and pray for.

Especially after a leather belt and the fear of God no longer seemed to curb his self-destructive ways.

So, she found someone that was capable of doing what she could not.

Enter stage left, a Mr. Bob Fucking Hatchet.

And now, thanks to his postmaster, the young man finally had the ability to take a firm stand against Harmony's Chief Prick.

From day one, that son-of-a-bitch has been tormenting every aspect of his life.

Since no murder had taken place at the postal carriers house, and they're not actually sure he's missing, the mail found at Dudley DoWright's "as he always does," was government property and not considered evidence of a crime scene.

Tommy demanded with as much ferocity a first-time cock-of-the-walk could muster, that not only did the Postal Service have full and legal rights to it ,but Mr. Hatchet better back the fuck off or he would reveal their dirty little secret like the Hen House had done concerning Tom, Mary, and John.

It was up to him, and him alone, to make sure every last piece of undelivered mail was finally received by its rightful owner or returned to the persons from whom it had been sent.

If Bob Hatchet, Harmony's Chief of Police had his way, he was going to burn every single letter, magazine, past due bill, and photographs that could be used against those who took them.

He was even willing to commit arson if that was his last and only option when it came to keeping his felony acts out of the hands of government officials.

Especially the Federal Bureau of Investigations.

For you see, even he had a place on Dudley's infamous wall.

The Little League Instructor was not happy that some of the items were pictures of him and his baseball team, the Chicken Hawks.

He's been their coach for over ten years now.

Thanks be to the Egyptian God Ra none of them were the nude ones that he had secretly snapped while his boys were skinny dipping in the home's back-yard pool.

Their parents had no earthly idea that when they dropped off their young men at Bob's house for his weekend pool parties, it was always sternly stressed that nudity was preferred but optional.

And because of their devotion to him, he would never withhold anything from them.

All the beer, drugs, and every type of porn a teenage kid could possibly ever want to consume, was readily made available to his precious boys.

Daddy Bob knew exactly how to love his young bucks.

Because their coach said it wouldn't be a problem since he was the chief of police and had the entire weekend off anyway, it was not unusual for them to call their parent's beggingly asking if they could possibly spend a night or two.

Just to keep him company, Coach Hatchet would sometimes call a few of his, "special," buddies over too.

Chief Bob had many male friends from across the globe with whom he would exchange videos, pictures, and every so often, one of his lost boy's.

With Sandra gone, the men could form their own private summer camp and spend the entire weekend nudely hanging out with the team.

As if the feds were always listening, Hatchet would use a special code by inviting them to a baseball game.

They just needed to bring their bat and balls.

Men against the boys.

And as always, clothing is optional.

Just knowing that they were the number one team to take state, for the last five years in a row, kept him and his rock-hard cock hungrily looking forward to that next seasons batch of budding young men who were willing to do whatever it took to get on his team.

And that willingness to do whatever it takes to be chosen sometimes came in a bow wrapped package from their parents.

He was so pleased with how well they could harbor a secret.

Especially the sixteen and over ones.

While he slept, he liked to keep them tied up in his bed at night.

Bob would have preferred them younger, but the legal age of consent in his state was sixteen. So, he always made sure to never break that golden rule so no one could ever accuse him of rape or child molestation.

Seems Tommy Dunn would argue otherwise.

When sleeping over at his place, grown men always sleep naked, was one of the coach's ten commandments.

He never seemed to mind when they would ask if they could climb in and snuggle while Bob nudely laid there hard as a rock while enjoying his favorite porn.

He was quite proud of how they could push past their fears and give in to curiosity.

The Chicken Hawks coach especially loved to show, watch, and physically help them when it came to instructing his brood on the proper ways of stroking a cock.

At an early age, Bob's father had taught him that what a loving and devoted Daddy does with his boy in private was a once in a lifetime love.

Also, no one could know about their passionate affection for each other.

Ever.

Because, if anyone was to ever find out, the authorities would put the little boy in an animal shelter and, like a rabid dog, euthanize his ass.

Sandra Hatchet, Bob's wife, eventually stopped, (SMACK), questioning why she would always be sent, (SMACK), to her mother's during the weekends of his team's baseball games.

For at least two days, anyways, she was not getting beat, (SMACK), or verbally abused, (SMACK).

And, he always seemed a bit calmer, (smack), after she returned on a Monday afternoon.

So, most of the time, because she really needed a break, Sandra did what he said and unquestionably went along with her abusive husband's demands.

Now, as Mrs. Hatchet was running her vacuum cleaner across the floor, its hum seemed to be accentuating that damned screaming of the cicadas.

Their combined clamoring was tumultuously reverberating deep within her migrained ear drums.

She hated cicadas.

This season was an extreme and overly abundant one.

In her lifetime, Sandra has never seen so many.

There had to be thousands, if not tens of thousands, on her doors, windows screens, back patio, fence, and lawn.

The cicadas had even forced the Hatchet's to shut down their pool.

Bob was not happy with that decision.

SMACK!

SMACK!

SMACK!

Thankfully, since the unspoken discovery at Dudley DoWright's, "as he always does," Bob hasn't hit her in days.

Well, maybe once or twice.

SMACK!

A continually ringing front doorbell didn't do her any favors either. Like the cicadas, its infernal buzzing added that extra punch, (SMACK), as Tommy pressed it long and hard.

He knew full well that Sandra was home and alone.

When Bob wasn't present and accounted for, no company, invited or not, was ever allowed to visit her.

That was the only way, other than the cameras and a SMACK, the dominating asshole could continuously make sure she didn't have a slip of the tongue.

No one was to know about the physically sadistic relationship that was horrendously being pounded into her on a daily basis.

SMACK!

SMACK!

SMACK!

Just like what Tommy's violent punches were currently doing to the homes doorbell.

SMACK!

SMACK!

SMACK!

Because Sandra was taking too long with a response, he was frustratingly pounding the shit out of it.

When Tommy Dunn finally got hired at Harmony's Post office, he was the lowest man on the totem pole.

He had been begging to work there for the past five years and was waiting, ever so patiently, for his application to be finally accepted.

Tommy always knew that before he could make that giant leap to financial freedom, someone would eventually have to quit, retire, or die.

And, in a small town such as Harmony, it was usually death that allowed a person to move on up into a higher position because god knows Dudley DoWright, "as he always does," and Joe Beth Redd weren't going anywhere any time soon.

But, with Dudley and Joe Beth now gone, he received not only an instant promotion and given a very important task, Tommy was also going to make more money.

He didn't know which of the three was better, going from sorter to postman before the Postmaster decided to hoppity hip it out of town for a week, receiving a substantial raise, or that he was the last man standing when it came time to sort and pick through the mess from Dudley DoWright's, "as he always does," sexually neurotic obsession.

He found that fiasco tacked to the missing man's now vacated, and soon to be rented by him, walls.

After a little bit of whitewash, Tommy was absolutely sure he was going to love this place.

He even considered keeping the sticky, red leather chair.

Because of the drag marks carved deep into the home's wooden floor from were Dudley dragged the recliner from room to room, most of the floors would have to be redone.

Even the rear legs of the butt-sitter were needing to be replaced.

After years of being tipped back and pulled from room to room, the furniture's bottom support blocks had been worn down to sheer nubbins.

So much so that the sex chairs seamen-soaked leather was just millimeters from scraping the home's wooden planks too.

Thankfully, the kitchen's flooring was still in perfect shape.

Since that area was designated as the room where the bills and other frivolous things were kept, Dudley never seemed to feel the need to bust one off in the cooking space.

When it came to redelivering the stolen property, Tommy Dunn fully understand that every last piece of mail was the property of the United States Postal Service and was to be sorted and handed back in person.

"According to Postmaster Garcia," if he had to open or repackage anything, its contents were none of his damned business.

So, don't go sticking your nose into someone else's private and personal affairs.

And, if he couldn't return it by hand, then no matter how many years it took Granny Smith to shuffle her trifling ass down here and retrieve it from her mailbox, it was the USPS's responsibility to make sure the parcel never left the building by any other means.

But hell, who would blame him if he took an accidental peak inside?

Since no one was left, no one would know.

They were either dead or missing.

In his hands were all the secrets of Harmony and their crooked Chief of Police.

A MR. BOB FUCKING HATCHET!

What more could a small petty thief want than being handed the keys to Pandoras box?

Her treasure chest contained the best form of blackmail anyone could ever want or ask for.

Screw the Hen House, "thought Harmony's newest mail carrier," they had nothing like this big shiny pot of gold he had found hidden at the end of Dudley DoWright's, "as he always does," rainbow.

Tommy Dunn knew Chief Bob hit Sandra.

SMACK!

Shit, he was a violent man and Daddy Bob has personally busted his plaything, (SMACK), on more than one occasion.

Unbeknownst to Tommy's mom, there was only one reason why Chief Hatchet never did throw Mr. Dunn permanently in jail.

Bob would rather have Tommy chained up in the playrooms sling back at his house than uselessly confined in one of the lockup cells down at his office.

He enjoyed slamming his throbbing manhood deep inside his boy's moist and warm toy box.

Tommy's muffled screams got him off every fucking time.

That's why, when Tommy arrived at Bob's house so that he could personally surrender what was found on Dudley's wall of shame, the reluctant bearer of bad news was still in a state of shock.

Instead of calling the Feds like they were supposed to, Mr. Garcia had ordered him to relinquish even the illegal stuff.

Tommy was to bundle, package, and redeliver it in a non-conspicuous box. And once he gave back the Chiefs property, including the videos, Mr. Dunn was to never speak of it again.

If the shoe had been on the other foot and he had been able to do what he really wanted, Tommy would have destroyed every ounce of incriminating evidence that was associated with him, the chief, and the horrible things that took place down in the man's basement.

Especially those fucking VHS tapes!

Just as he was about to ring their doorbell for the last and final time, Tommy realized that Daddy's secret box, as requested by Chief Bob, was supposed to be personally delivered to their local police station by no one other than Tommy.

Bull shit, the man with the power grumbled.

And after deciding his game plan, the postman came up with the perfect response once he was cornered and questioned by Mr. you know who.

Tommy would answer the same way his mom would continually quote when he did something she didn't like or approve of.

Whatever.

As he continued to stand there, Mr. Dunn knew Sandra was home and just trying her best to ignore him.

After all the years of receiving Chief Bob's special rewards, "as Daddy liked to call it," he figured it was about time to return the favor.

Seems that unbeknownst to Sandra Beth, Mr. Dunn had decided to use his newly founded authority and personally share this treasure chest containing some of Bob's most bountiful riches with Mrs. Hatchet.

On her husband's behalf, the abused housewife will be receiving the award for willful ignorance to kidnapping and felonious acts of a violent and sexual nature against unwilling and unsuspecting participants between the ages of thirteen to sixteen.

They were the best pirated revenge one could ever ask or dream for.

Sandra had to have known what was going on.

He was committing these heinous acts right under her nose.

While sequestered in Bob's dungeon, there were many days that he could hear the woman's sobs and muffled cries while she vacuumed and cleaned the homes main floor.

However, she did and she didn't.

Upon returning from her mothers, the vanquished spouse knew about the boys on his team because of their destructive aftermath but she never had an inkling Mr. Dunn was or had been there too.

The battered woman considered Tommy one of her favorite people to talk with and would never do anything to purposely harm or deceive him.

On more than one occasion, they would randomly run into each other.

Usually at their local Post Office.

Unlike most of the women and men around these parts, he was always polite, respectable, and treated her like a lady.

However, like the rest of the town's residents, she was pretty sure the kid also knew what Bob was doing to her behind closed doors.

SMACK!

When out and about, Sandra always wore the largest pair of sunglasses money could buy.

She was never seen without them.

Mrs. Hatchet used those gawdy things to constantly hide the massive shiners Bob would give her.

SMACK!

SMACK!

Most of the time, they generally appeared when she would loudly protest about having to go and spend another long and drawn-out weekend at her elderly mother's place.

SMACK!

Really, how could a gal bitch so much?

Especially with a pair of busted lips.

SMACK!

SMACK!

Thankfully, she wasn't made to leave every damned weekend.

He only enforced her departure during baseball season and those special moments Bob would say he needed her to leave so he could spend some private and quality time with his buddies.

SMACK!

SMACK!

At an early age, his Daddy taught him that an excessively hard SMACK would help keep a rocky marriage from falling apart.

Son, if she's scared to breathe, she's scared to leave.

Now hit the bitch.

SMACK!

SMACK!

SMACK!

A prophecy Sandra Beth was hoping to one day prove false.

Mrs. Hatchet might not have been there for the clothing optional festivities, but it was what the oppressed homemaker returned too that got her goat.

A house full of rowdy, rough housing boy's running in and out, while eating every single piece of junk food in sight.

Untold bags of trash.

Half-eaten food.

And sinks full of unwashed dishes.

All being spurred on by her no-good husband!

Their drunk coach was encouraging them to act like godless hooligans.

Seems every male there, loved to take turns destroying anything and everything that was either Sandra's or considered precious to her.

The team made such a large mess of clutter and chaos, the hoarder producers from that dramatic show would most likely have given her an audition.

There were a few other things that burnt her popcorn also.

That disaster came from what was always waiting to greet her the second Bob's wife stepped just outside their backdoor.

Who would blame her for getting angry?

A yard full of pool accessories, spilt alcohol, and, "every now and then," one or two of the boys swimming trunks and underwear.

They were always scattered randomly around the house, their bedroom and bathrooms.

She used to ask Bob why the boys would leave their clothes in their personal quarters, but the answer to that question was always the same.

SMACK!

Some of his boys were really shy and didn't want to bathe with their team members who were already in the process of cleaning up in the spare lavatory.

And why did you allow that, she asked?

His final response to that question shut her right the fuck up.

Boys will be boys.

SMACK!

And don't you question my decisions or motives ever again.

SMACK!

SMACK!

SMACK!

As the home's doorbell continuously rang, her intense and overpowering headache began to work itself into every square inch of her body and mind.

The last time Harmony's battered victim experienced such a splitting headache was after putting her foot down when it came to hosting a pool party for his team while the cicadas continuously plagued the area.

There's no way we can do that Bob, she insisted.

The flying bombers make it completely impossible for someone to sit out there and enjoy themselves.

You can barely see the cement as it is.

Look for yourself.

And boy did he.

That break your husband's heart mistake costed Sandra dearly.

SMACK!

SMACK!

SMACK!

SMACK!

SMACK!

SMACK!

A look for yourself proclamation that was going to cost her dearly once again.

When Mrs. Hatchet finally gave in and decided to peak out the window, there stood Tommy Dunn. He was holding one of the largest packages she could ever remember being delivered to their house.

For some reason, Tommy seemed to have the biggest, shit eating grin on his face.

This Cheshire cat had a secret and was hoping Sandra wanted to play a game of guess what's in the box?

Winner takes all.

He would even toss in a free ball of red packaging string.

Back at his office, Chief Hatchet had just gotten off the phone with Dan.

He was angered over the fact that Tommy Dunn would not turn over the evidence to his office before any of the contents from the house of the still missing postal carrier could be delivered to its rightful owners.

On top of that, He was also wondering why his package has not arrived yet?

To his horror, all special deliveries from Dudley's former residence were being hand delivered to the senders last known address.

And as he started to complain, Garcia wouldn't even give him time to explain what was going on or to address the Chief's irrational concerns about Don's newest employee.

Mr. Garcia's only response to the pissed off officer was that Mr. Dunn was in charge and would be making all the decisions.

To save face, the Postal Service was personally apologizing to those that had been affected by Dudley's illegal acts.

So, when it came to getting the job done right, Harmony's Postmaster had all the confidence he needed in Tommy.

Either way, he had to go.

The Mayor and Pastor West were deciding on how best to slip their poles into Anna's fishing holes at the exact same time. They were busily working on how to rhythmically hit that sweet spot without him, Garcia stressed.

So their catch doesn't panic or try to get away from them, he needed to immediately give the two men a helping hand.

And right before he hung up, because of all the huffing and puffing going on in the background, it sounded like the fishing was really good to a still fuming and perplexed Hatchet.

CH 8.
UMPIRE, UMPIRE, WE NEED AN UMPIRE.

For all the years Chief Bob has been in law enforcement, there has never been a person or situation he could not handle due to his overwhelming size.

He is a very large bear of a man.

Six foot seven, to be exact.

Once a person was in his custody, even the hardest of criminals were intimidated.

His booming voice and muscular brick walled frame carried such a demeanor of assuredness and confidence even a four-star general would sit up and take notice.

When Helen walked into his office to ask about the new sex crimes file he just opened, his shocked appearance completely took her by surprise.

Bob's face had not only drained of all color, but the imposing giant couldn't even muster up enough strength to answer in his normally deep, demanding, I'm taking charge now voice.

Instead, it came out in a raspy, dying last breath kind of way.

All the chief could squeakily say was a vehemently and almost inaudible, I'm going to kill the son of a bitch, before furiously jumping up and bounding for the door.

The desk Bob used weighed well over three hundred pounds.

And because of the furniture's behemoth size, it was practically impossible for Helen to budge it on her own for even just an inch.

But, as her boss bolted from the room, Chief Bob ended up shoving it over five feet across his office floor.

Believe me, Ms. Dunn would say, when sweeping and mopping his office, that things a beast. So, how was she supposed to push it back into place by herself?

Because of the way he bolted out of this place, Helen was sure someone must have found Sandra Hatchet's bloodied and beaten to death body.

As Harmony's Chief sped home, Nora Toliver, who just happened to be standing outside the town's only bed and breakfast that day, observed the Officer doing no less than eighty miles an hour.

Bob decided if Sandra had opened any of his package before he got home, she was going to be beat down once again.

SMACK!

SMACK!

SMACK!

The last time his wife had accidentally snooped in his mail, she had, (SMACK, SMACK), received two black eyes that day.

Do to its contents, he might even kill her this time.

SMACK!

And, if anyone just happened to ask about Sandra's sudden disappearance, he would say that she finally left him about a month or so ago.

Supposedly, she's moved in with her mother, about eight feet under his new pool pad, somewhere deep down in the Florida Keys.

Tommy may not believe him and possibly get curious enough to snoop around, but Daddy has a special place in mind for that boy.

If need be, he wouldn't have an issue keeping his toy indefinitely tied up and prostituted to those who could afford the hefty price that was required when it came to a hands-on playdate with the viral prodigy.

Unbeknownst to Mr. Dunn, he was the infamous child star of a show called, Guess what time it is: It's Tommy Time.

An illegal, how to train your submissive tutorial being broadcast on the Dark Web

And even though they were introduced to the little tyke that very first day his mother gave him to the Chief, he and Daddy didn't submissively start training and entertaining its pedophile creepers until the boy officially turned sixteen.

And now, due to Tommy's let's start some shit actions, Harmony's Alpha Master was needing to discipline his kid once more.

Thankfully, he was the only thread needing to be clipped concerning the skeletons in the law officer's closet.

Other than Mary Parker, who was now dead and buried, no one really cared about getting to personally know Sandra or come between her and Bobs lethal back hand.

SMACK!

What the Hells that screaming noise, Bob Hatchet mind numbingly pondered?

While racing home, he had forgotten about turning on his sirens. They were not only blasting at their highest setting possible, but an extremely large number of cicadas had gotten into his cruiser also.

And do to their combined efforts, the never-ending wailing was really starting to give him a splitting headache.

He had to wonder if Sandra would even be there stewing patiently for him to get home, or had she picked up their phone and called those who handled such horrific matters by now.

Either way, she'd be dead before they got to him.

Earlier, while waiting for her husband to arrive home, Sandra was trying to decide whether or not to run or, for once in her life, fight the bastard.

The box full of smut that was addressed to her husband had been retrieved from Dudley DoWright's, "as he always does," house.

She had no idea that her husband, this side of the Mississippi, was considered the King of pedophilia.

He was the largest distributer of child pornography the United Sates Government has ever seen.

For close to ten years now, the Federal Bureau of Investigation were actively searching for his base of operations.

So, at this point, it really didn't matter what she did with the box. Sandra has probably seen its contents by now and that leaves her husband with only one disciplinary option.

She has to be killed.

SMACK!

SMACK!

BANG!

BANG!

DEAD.

DEAD.

Thus, saith god?

THUS, SAITH BOB!

Before the Government Official showed up at Chief Bob's home, he did the one thing all United States Postal Service workers were forbidden to do.

He decided to stop at his house first, grab a box cutter, and take a quick peak inside.

It was probably in his best interest after all; because, not only did it contain pictures pertaining to child porn, but there were also a few videos about him.

MY SPECIAL BOY.

THE LIFE AND TIMES OF TOMMY.

Every time Chief Hatchet would arrest him, he would threaten Tommy with a month in jail or a weekend in Daddy's playroom.

Mr. Dunn had no idea that everything taking place in Candyland was being recorded.

Not only was he doing that, Daddy Hatchet was also producing and distributing copies across the entire northern and southern hemispheres of the Americas.

Sales that also stretched across the European Union.

It could not have taken but thirty or forty minutes after Tommy dropped off that special package, before Sandra heard the sirens come wailing up their street.

As what to do with all of Bob's collection of child porn, she had decided to keep possession of it until she could decide which option was best.

Should she stay and fight, his heinous actions may never be revealed.

But, if she chose to flee instead, Sandra knew the subject matter in this box would be the only things that guarantee her safety until she could be relocated after the time came to punish him for the years of bruises, beatings, and broken bones her fraudulent husband has torturously inflicted on her.

There was no doubt that Bob was going to physically destroy her this time.

SMACK!

Possibly to the point of deaths door.

SMACK!

Or maybe, just maybe, he was finally going to kill her.

If she was lucky, he would just kick her ass to the curb.

SMACK!

And hopefully, for the last and final time, Sandra would be sent to her sweet and elderly mother with only a couple of blackened eyes this go around.

SMACK!

SMACK!

As she daydreamed on, the screeching of Bob's tires out in front of their house propelled Sandra from the migraines foggy red haze.

While fully engulfed in the deluge of what ifs, the abused spouse had subconsciously grabbed the little league coaches' favorite aluminum bat.

Sandra has never swung a baseball bat or any other kind of sports equipment used for pummeling an inanimate object.

But, there has to be a first time for everything.

And because of what was about to occur, Mrs. Hatchet understood that the time to do such a thing was finally here.

With its solid metal end slamming across his pedophilic face, the beaten down housewife hoped that she would have enough time to great Mr. Monster at their front door.

Sadly, Bob, to her detriment, had other ideas.

It was not the front door he entered.

After years in law enforcement, an officer quickly learns that one never goes running through the main entrance of an occupied structure.

When it came to subduing the criminal, or criminals they had been sent to capture for their monthly required collar, stealth was your saving grace.

And why is that Officer Hatchet?

Because every good cop knows that the very second anyone's head begins to peek around the corner for a better layout of the Land, you can always guarantee someone is on the other side and just waiting to blow it the fuck off.

Sandra never stood a snowball's chance in Hell.

Especially when he saw her cowering behind the front door with his favorite implement.

A torturous instrument Tommy Dunn knew all too well.

After seeing her weapon of choice, Bob quickly decided that what's good for the goose, is good for the gander.

So, before cautiously slithering through their back-door screen, Bod grabbed his second favorite bat from the leagues equipment bag still sitting by the patio's rear door.

LET THE BALLGAMES BEGIN, YELLED THE ANNOUNCER!

In average, the human body contains approximately six liters of blood.

Before she finally collapsed, Bob figured after his first two or three swings, (SMACK, SMACK, SMACK), he must have knocked at least one liter from Sandra's ruptured skull.

And while the homemaker's attacker stood there admiring his handywork, her husband, (SMACK), watched the rest of Sandra's pitiful and subdued life slowly drain across the cream-colored rooms checker tiled floor.

SMACK!

SMACK!

SMACK!

The Fourier's egg-shell white vibe was no longer white in any form or appearance.

Fresh blood splattered every aspect of the greeting room's ceiling, two walls, the interior entrance's double doors, windows, and frame.

And, Mr. Bob Fucking Hatchet.

Crumpled at the attackers feet, were the unrecognizable remains of Sandra Hatchet.

His, "until death do us part," wife.

The new bride should have trusted her mother's instincts and took a moment to read the fine print first before signing and saying, Yes I Do.

Seems that when it came time for Bob to say yes to the same clause she did, he signed something entirely different.

Unbeknownst to the newly blushing bride, he interpreted that declaration of love entirely different.

She was now his to do with as he pleases.

If he hits her, he hits her.

If he beats her, he beats her.

And if he just so happens to kill her.

He kills her.

And he absolutely meant it.

Laying at her killer's blood-soaked feet were the battered remains of a headless woman.

The abused victim was sprawled out on her back and saturated in an ever-expanding pool of blood plus pulverized brain matter while shattered skull fragment scattered throughout the obliterated aftermath of the future Jane Doe slowly drifted across the still creeping liquid.

And that's when the hand of death reached out and touched Mr. Dunn's soul.

Daddy Hatchet mindlessly mumbled a most horrible prediction.

You're next Tommy Boy.

You're next.

Hatchet was going to dispose of his and Sandra's bodies the same way he had disposed of the Sodomite Mark Padden that had been so righteously killed by Mr. Parker.

Of course, the paperwork concerning any proof of their physical existence of ever being or living in Harmony will somehow have end up misfiled, lost, or accidently tossed in the Trash-Doe-Can.

As the stunned postal carrier continued to look-on, about three liters of the gooey ooze was beginning to spread across the six-by-eights front entrance.

A greeting area not so welcoming anymore, the stunned peeping tom thought while trying not to pass out from the shock-and aw of what just happened.

Then it hit him.

If the law enforcer was willing to kill his very own wife, the newly declared Pedophilic Emperor of Bird-Land would have no issues killing him too.

And that's when Tommy Dunn's balls finally dropped.

The time had come to man-up.

If he was meant to be killed by this man, then he was going to decide the time and place of his possible demise.

And after what he just witnessed; now seems to be the time, and this seems to be the place.

Earlier in the day, after he finished delivering the large box to Bob Hatchet's residential home, Tommy wasn't sure if it was a good idea to stick around and see what happens.

Almost, that was.

Now, after witnessing what just happened, Daddy's play-toy suddenly wished he had listened to his own advice.

Tommy had no idea that today was the last time he would get to visit with Sandra Hatchet ever again.

He sure knows know, yes he does.

He sure knows now.

The Chief had been sprinting across his backyard in such a blind haste, that he never did see Tommy Dunn hiding in the shrubs underneath the stained-glass window of their newly remodeled kitchen.

Daddy Hatchet had no fucking clue that in just a moment, like Sandra's, his noggin would be knocked out of the park too.

SMACK!

All at the hands of his Dark-Webbed Allstar.

BATTER UP, YELLED THE UMPIRE!

Seems Tommy Dunn decided to go out in style after announcing that he was retiring from the Chicken Hawks. And his final time at bat just so happened to be the home-run Tommy needed.

SMACK!

ITS TOMMY DUNN, CRIES ANNOUNCER NUMBER TWO.

TOMMY DUNN IS NOW UP TO BAT.

CH 9.
KILL THE BASTARD.

Since Bob had his back turned and seemed to be more preoccupied with his handywork than his surroundings, he never noticed the spectator or the horrified look on Tommy's face as he stood there peering in the homeowner's kitchen window while the officer took that first swing, (SMACK), and cracked Sandra's skull wide open.

The gush of blood and brain matter that exploded across the room reminded the sexually abused victim of when Moses in that old movie called the Ten Commandments, lifted his staff and proceeded to split the red sea.

One side of her skull went this way.

And the other side of Sandra's cranium went that way.

And just as the sea did in Cecil B. Demille's cinematic masterpiece, her head instantly split wide open.

NEXT BATTER, YELLES THE COACH!

The Chicken Hawk's commander never saw Tommy grab another persuader from the equipment bag.

To save his own ass, Tommy Dunn dropped Bob Hatchet like a jail house snitch drops a dime on another inmate.

It was done and over with before he ever knew what hit him.

As Tommy reached for the outfield's fence, his first swing slammed across the back of Bob's skull.

SMACK!

The force from that impact split the teams wooden club right in half.

HOME RUN, YELLES THE TEAM!

Before Bob Hatchet was beaten into unconscious submission, (SMACK) Tommy Dunn asked him a very serious and deadly question.

Daddy, have you ever been the star of a snuff film?

SMACK!

Of course you haven't.

SMACK!

Well, as of today, that will no longer be the case.

SMACK!

Your infamous actions are about to go viral.

SMACK!

SMACK!

SMACK!

TOMMY DUNN WINS, YELLES THE CROWD!

Making sure to close all the curtains in the lawman's house after Daddy Bob was securely tied up, Tommy sat down and for the first time ever, began to watch every video that had his name written on them.

Again.

And again.

And again.

The young man couldn't believe that this demon from Hell had filmed all of his nasty, dirty little obsessions he had committed on, in, and with him.

Seems the King of child porn had also recorded those sadistically perverse things he made Tommy do with his favorite minions.

Those were the ones who followed, paid for, and were personally invited to taste and play with the Sultan of Sadomasochism and his treasured concubine.

A costly adventure the lovers of young men reserved with an abated ferocity.

The anything goes orgies were the worst.

So, after tearing every inch of that infamous bordello apart, and thanks to an extra burst of unhinged rage from remembering all the times he was forcibly gang raped, it didn't take the sexually trafficked victim much longer before he found Daddy's well-hidden cameras.

And once he turned the recorders back on, Tommy made sure all ten of them were aimed directly at the leather sling.

When he was tied up, Daddy Hatchet would force him into spending unfathomable hours, days, and a few weeks now and then, nudely hanging gagged and bound in the domination accessory.

Mr. Dunn abhorred that torturous contraption.

So, once the scene was staged, the Dark-Web Star began his once in a lifetime broadcast to the entire World Wide Web.

And it's Free.

At the hands of his victim, it was going to be the first, LIVE, FROM THE PLAYROOM, broadcast of what the sexual predator did to him.

Anyone and everyone who wanted to log in and get off, was invited to watch a captured pedophile finally get what's coming to them.

While revealing the evidence documenting his tortured past, the young man hosting this segment was going to recreate the perpetrator's physical and sexual brutalization that had been forced upon his unwilling victim.

His abuser was going to help Tommy demonstrate the torturous horrors that were inflicted on him.

And for those who stay till the end, their reward would be the monsters snuff film debut.

Today, in Harmony, Tommy Dunn and the townships Chief of Police, a Mr. Bob Fucking Hatchet, were about to make History.

Unbeknownst to him, the timid young man was about to become a God. And like his favorite comic book characters, he was about to live forever in infamy.

Everyone on this big blue marble would never, ever, forget Tommy Dunn's name.

Three.

Two.

One.

Action.

Tommy made sure that before sacrificing Chief Bob's life, he would host a show and tell hour.

Just like they had to do in elementary school.

Every single thing that had been done to Sandra, the local children from his baseball team, the Chicken Hawks, and to Tommy Dunn himself, was broadcast across the internet.

That's the entire mother fucking internet, a newscaster later exclaimed.

Only thing was, the other recorded men involved in these illegal escapades always made sure to cover their faces.

So, Tommy made a plea.

After hopefully breaking free from their sadistically dominating Daddies, just like Tommy did, it would be the other trapped boys responsibility to expose their own Daddy's nasty little secrets.

That very day, Tommy should have patented the videos title and claimed an internet domain by the same name.

It's beloved popularity quickly surpassed any and all porn sites and instantaneously became the worlds most watched program.

Seems people from across the globe were officially fed up with pedophiles.

They were tired of grown ass adults, especially men, taking up positions of authority so they could be closer to kids.

Enough was enough!

Society was no longer going to stand by and willfully allow God's innocent children to be molested.

Especially when it came to their own miserable heathens.

If this is what it took to stop them, then so be it.

Who knew or could have even guessed that within a few short months, Tommy's program would become the entire planets number one reality show on cable television.

TURN YOUR DADDY IN!

THE SHOW & TELL HOUR.

In a small town like Harmony, there are entire days were nothing happens.

Helen Dunn, Bob's personal secretary, was so glad when Daddy decided to spend the money and have the internet installed on the computer in his private office.

Whenever Bob had to split for some unforeseen reason, she finally had something to do during those long, dead and boring hours that Harmony seemed to endlessly heap upon its local law enforcement.

As Ms. Dunn surfed the net, she accidentally stumbled across a live voyeur sight that lets you see what other people are doing in the privacy of their own homes.

And it was free.

So, after clicking the I'm twenty-one verification button, Tommy's live cam show was the first to pop up on the Chief's computer screen.

Seems over one-million viewers and counting, were currently logged into the reveal and executionary broadcast of the man who coached a Little League team that goes by the name Chicken Hawks.

A term of endearment used by sexually deviant men to describe their preference for young boys and men who still possessed the appearance of pre-pubescent adolescents.

The pedophile was found guilty of the most heinous crimes.

The grooming, sodomizing, and sexual trafficking of children.

At first, it puzzled Helen as to why her son would purposely state that he was broadcasting from Bob Hatchet's house.

Harmony's Chief of Police.

He was also the man she had chosen to mentor her boy.

Just as the recently deputized dispatcher was about to reach for the mike and call for back up at the Chiefs place, forgetting that John Bishop was now dead, her one and only son took a deep breath, looked straight into the cameras, and said these words.
ARE YOU READY?

GUESS WHAT TIME IT IS?

IT'S THAT TIIME!

TIME TO TURN YOUR DADDY IN.

THE SHOW & TELL HOUR.

And after seeing the chapter recorded the day he officially turned sixteen, THE WICKED ADVENTURES OF TOMMY, COACH, AND FIFTEEN OF COACHE'S DEVIENT FRIENDS, Helen decided that it wasn't in their best interest to involve any other law enforcement.

So, before someone could possibly respond from the next town over, Ms. Dunn hung up the receiver, grabbed the handgun in her purse, and headed out for Bob's place.

She would do whatever it took to save Tommy.

Even if that meant killing the fucking-bastard.

Most people love the rain and it's smells.

They particularly love how it soothingly feels against their body's sunbaked skin when falling from a broiling summers sky. Especially those individuals who are working outside and suffering from the sun's dehydrating effects.

For all to observe, they endlessly implore the Gods to ease their pain and suffering.

These individuals always appear to be looking skyward while begging and pleading to whatever God or God's they outwardly perceive to pray and worship too.

Seems that for even just a drop of thirst-quenching water, they are willing to barter the lives of their own damned children.

Others like the way rain washes away dirt, grime, and any other proof of evidence someone might be trying to bury or hide in their backyard gardens.

Helen knew that it wouldn't be long now before her fucking employer would also be begging Tommy and Ms. Dunn for relief.

Yes, Helen decided that after they got back into town, it was time to take her sweet and sexually abused boy down into Harmony's apple grove before those next flood drenching storms moved in.

And, with any luck, their downpours would hush the Cicada's plague of mind-numbing noise and help wash away all evidence from the mother and son's own blood-stained hands.

Those logged in and searching the black web of cyber space were parched for rain. And thanks to Tommy Dunn, their prayers for something to drink had finally been answered by the most glorious type of entertainment.

A show involving death.

TURN YOUR DADDY IN!

THE SHOW AND TELL HOUR.

In less than a twenty-four-hour period, the site had received over one billion hits.

It seemed as if every individual who could possibly be interested in such things, tried their damndest to copy and share its contents before the web sites could remove the explicit program.

The viral telecast quickly became the most sought-after video ever.

The live transmission of a pedophile being executed caused the entire internet to crash. Not one server from across the globes four corners escaped the downloading onslaught intact.

After all these years, Daddy's abused boys decided it was time for their own videos.

They were also wanting their tormentors to see, feel, and understand just how much his love had meant to them and figured the time had finally come to give back.

Within days of Tommy's last performance, other boy toys who had somehow managed to break free from their captors, began to make their guest appearance on the popular sight.

They would also take the implements of destruction that had been mercilessly shoved inside them and use these behemoths to destroy the tormentor's ass too.

Most Daddies keep these ridiculously large ass-busters within arm's reach.

And why is that, pray-tell?

Because, one never knows when the desire to scratch that ass stretching itch might hit.

And after finding what they were searching for, the former prey would then do a live broadcast of their adventure also. Just like their Idol Tommy Dunn did, on cables number one rated show.

Five years and counting.

At first, there were those who protested.

But, it quickly became apparent the men were nambla members and trying to stop the program before their boys made them publicly answer and pay for the sins committed against children under the consenting age of eighteen.

ARE YOU READY?

WHAT TIME IS IT?

IT'S THAT TIME!

TIME TO TURN YOUR DADDY IN.

THE SHOW AND TELL HOUR.

With Founders Day fast approaching, the apple grove was securely locked up.

It would not be available to the public until the ribbon cutting ceremony could take place on opening day.

Until Abenaki's arrival, the orchard had been completely abandoned and was off limits to any and every-one.

It only took five years of gossip and backstabbing amongst the towns council, before she and the Hen House finally received permission to restore Harmony's orchard, cider mill, and distribution of apple trees amongst the city's main streets.

And because of their combined efforts, Founders Day would be celebrated by its residents once again.

Abenaki quickly realized that after just a few short weeks of moving into town, these people are not only nuts, but they were fucking nuts.

There also seemed to be a few of them who's elevator definitely didn't reach the top floor.

Helen Dunn was quite surprised to find Dudley DoWright. "as he always does," just hanging around by his lonesome once she and her cohort reached the massive apple tree that was growing in the dead center of the municipality's apple grove.

No one has been able to locate him since Joe and Sue Beth Redd were found murdered and locked inside the post office.

Anyone who was a local yokel and knowing full well of the towns secret and hidden past, never really wanted to hang out in this cursed place anyway.

And when they finally accepted the fact that he was nowhere to be found amongst Harmony's residential population, the search for Dudley DoWright, "as he always does," quickly came to an end.

Just like it will once Helen and Tommy are declared missing too.

Especially since there was no one left to look.

Just like he and his mom, they are probably dead, dying, or about to be.

******

CH 10.
A LEAP OF FAITH.

In the year eighteen-forty of our Lord and Savior Jesus Christ, Johnathon Tucker, while watching the most exquisite sunrise ever seen, stoically stood over their newly established town of Harmony.

He couldn't help but feel that their one and only god was protectively watching over them.

But, no sooner than it had peaked into their valley, the blackest of sky's, just like Jonathon's heart, began to block both of their views.

He was quite surprised, because one usually doesn't see such turbulence until late spring to mid-summer and hoped that the severe thunderstorms wouldn't violently flood the new, still to be built, town.

They were rolling and boiling like a fresh batch of searing tar.

That special kind of thickness needed to patch roofs. Or, if need be, tar and feather some dumb ass sinner who always seemed to be deserving of such righteous punishment.

Father Johnathon felt like he could literally reach out and touch them as that mornings now obscured sun began its ascent from behind the mountain protecting their valley and across the northern Rockies.

Thankfully, he knew the heavy rains would soon come and wash away all traces from that nights irreproachable cleansing of their god promised land.

Thus, saith god?

THUS, SAITH JOHNATHON.

What had they done?

Here he stands amongst the Founding Fathers, just on the outskirts of where Harmony's future house of worship and town settlement will be located, solemnly staring over the shrub lined ridge into the smaller valley below.

It was Johnathon's fainting vision at the altar which sent the entire congregation into a frenzied state of packing the wagons, before god could possibly change his mind and send another congregation who was more obedient, out into the wilderness.

Johnathon prophesied that, "GOD SAID," their new home would be growing with the most delicious fruit trees and be the promised land the Protestants' had been fasting and praying for.

And once they arrived, the unquestionable Deity wanted his new city to be built on a very large ridge located between two mountains.

The settlement needed to be constructed at that exact location so it could overlook and protect Eden's garden.

Harmony's diameter would be measured out at about five full blocks in width and a quarter-mile in length. Below his holy establishment, down in its valley, God would plant the perfect apple orchard anyone could possibly ask or beg for.

Itself, about two blocks in circumference.

A small, waist deep river always full of the winters sweetest snow melt would flow in a perfect horseshoe bend, about half a block in width, around the raised thicket of fruit trees.

When spring comes, its waters would flood their little valley orchard, depositing a thick layer of sand and silt upon the land, and feed the roots of their trees with the most heavenly forms of manna.

This blessing would create an exotically unusual, and extremely addicting flavor of mouthwatering fruit.

What more could an apple tree ask for, but to have its roots firmly anchored deep just in case spring rains unexpectedly brought flash floods while drinking year-round from the sweetest mountain water God has ever blessed his creation with.

As the storms began to rage, Johnathon couldn't help but wonder if the blood dripping from his fingertips would somehow stain Harmony's Hallowed Grounds.

Would God forgive him and the other men standing at the cliff's shrubbed lined edge who were also crying and quietly kneeling by his side.

They, like him, were still dressed in attire that was soaked with the blood of those who were just killed for the land bequeathed to them by god.

Just like Moses and the Israelites had been ordered to do when they came to take the land, he and the Fathers slaughtered every last man, boy, and animal.

Graciously, it only took a matter of hours instead of the forty years it took them because of the tribes incompetence to follow orders.

Thus, saith god?

THUS, SAITH JOHNATHON.

Johnathon knew that the only way to destroy a pagan's teachings, before any of them could possibly pass on such Witch Doctor Voodoo, was to kill every last savage.

A conclave of opposing beliefs he assumed to have been successfully removed from their hallowed grounds.

And now, because of what he was currently hearing, Johnathon understood he and the men were not done yet.

They still had work to do.

For some reason, as the tribal elders shared their history, the story telling always came with flutes, beating drums, and obnoxiously wailing women.

He kind of missed that rhythm.

But, to his bewilderment, ever so softly and ever so slowly, the drums once again began to beat from the overlooked women and girls who had, as if by magic, been obscured from God's judgment.

The mother's suffering response to the tribes men and their sons being killed seemed to arouse the cicadas.

The bugs were so loud that Johnathon could have sworn the pounding headache settling between the pastor's eardrums was being created by his own beating heart and not those infernal wails from the cicada's and the women who survived the congregations initial attack.

At first, he even considered that the searing pain trying to crack his walnut was caused from the rush and excitement of last night's raid.

However, on the flip side of things, the droning had such a soothing reverberation.

The air, as if alive, was literally vibrating from their combined spirits.

Because their husbands and sons had been unnecessarily slaughtered, the lamenting women's voices, accompanied by the cicada's cries, began to menacingly rise up from the valleys blood-stained floor.

It felt as if the voices wailing its haunting melody were somehow possessed.

They were calling out for the hand of death, which rapes the depth of a man's soul before he violently rips it out from his still beating heart, to come and avenge them.

The howling from their women and children who were somehow left to bury their dead, melded ever so gracefully with the cicadas song.

As its musical intoxication began to consume the residents and their newly founded town of Harmony, Father Johnathon's blood began to run colder than a witch's tit in a cast iron bra.

He chalked up this reaction to their success and not to what was yet to happen down in their valley.

Because of their horrendous actions, the group of Christian refugees were no longer a hid behind the walls of fear settlement.

Instead, they were finally an established township now.

This would be where his children could now grow old and have families of their own.

Yes sir, god was definitely with them this morning.

A few nights before, the men of Johnathon's flock had gathered together and unanimously agreed on which plan of action they were going to take concerning those who were currently occupying their apple grove.

Because of the congregations selfless love and undying devotion, god himself said that they could seize the valley. And since this was to be their land, the unbelievers down below had to be dealt with.

When Moses and the former Egyptian slaves entered their promised land, God commanded that they were to kill every man, woman, and child.

Even the animals were to be sacrificed.

An order the roaming fanatics claimed to have received also.

So no evil could pervert their faith and beliefs, bringing sin into the hearts of their Protestant children, Harmony's Holy Grounds, just like Israel's, had to be cleansed before they could claim and occupy it.

That's why, just before the witching hour a few weeks after their arrival, the Fathers of Harmony snuck into the heathens sleeping camp and began to cleanse God's land of all disbelievers.

No wonder Moses, the Jewish nation, and the destitute of Egypt couldn't do it.

When it came to men, elders, animals, and boys, the Fathers didn't have an issue doing what they were told. However, when it came to the opposite sex, they had no idea just how impossible it would be to kill grandmothers, mothers, and girls.

The death of a helpless female was asking way too much from a loving and devoted Father.

Thus, saith god?

THUS, SAITH JOHNATHON.

As the sun rose upon that first cleansing day, Harmony's residents awoke to an unoccupied apple grove. Its beauty was no longer tainted or obscured by the wild ones illicit occupation.

What a glorious sight for every Protestant man, woman, and child when they saw that it was now made anew.

Fresh air brought up from the cleansed valley filled their lungs with the smell of glacier water, sweet grass, and a hint of apple cider.

That mornings dew, on the tips of every weary tongue, finally soothed their dry and parched souls.

The wide and stretched out ridge before them that first night of their arrival, begged the traveling band of Fathers to sit and rest for a spell.

Johnathon felt in his spirit that maybe, just maybe, this was finally the place.

He needed to stop, look around, and see what this specific ridge and valley had to offer. It was prophesied that the ground would beg them to walk its cliff faced edge and see what the Lord has done.

Not only would the traveling believers find a horseshoe bend river wrapping around an orchard down in a smaller valley below. Its blessed crop could be collected and consumed by their township also.

And this time around, god guaranteed that he would not only let them all live with his magnificent creation in Harmony, he also promised not to kick anyone out of the oasis because someone ate the formally forbidden fruit.

And there they were!

Eden's Garden and those divine apple trees of knowledge.

Could this actually be their promised land?

Before god's Founding Fathers could ever lay a corner stone, the ones who plagued this land like an infection that refuses to go away, had to be cut out first.

It was what their holy god commanded!

That was the only way he would even consider them as his blessedly chosen.

Like them, Moses and the children should have done what they were ordered to do. But sadly, because of their disobedience, Israel now has to live with the consequences of their disobedient ways.

Johnathon often wondered when and if they get to heaven, would Yahweh look at the Israelites and say these words.

I told you so, but you refused to believe me.

Because the eagles who flew with the Great Spirits started to cry out when the haggard group first arrived, tribesmen who lived upon the valleys floor began to look skyward.

They were wondering why the ancestors were crying out in such distress.

And to their shock and horror, white men were looking down upon them from their ancestral burial grounds above.

When someone in the tribe passed away, they would place their loved ones remains amongst the holy eagles above. It was a spiritual place where those left behind could visit with the remnants of an ancestor while reaching out to touch the sky.

It was believed that when seeking guidance and protection, the eagles would carry their prayers to that loved one living in the afterlife.

And if they were blessed enough to be heard, the spirit-bird would return with an answer.

As Johnathon approached the cliffs edge, he just couldn't believe what he was seeing. What appeared to be a place of burial was nothing more than a macabre of rotting flesh and trinkets.

Placed about six feet above the ground were the physical remains of their dead.

Their bodies were just tossed out like a pile of trash amongst the carnivorous birds.

And as they finished decomposing, what was left of their fleshy remains was eagerly snatched up and consumed by the vulturous raptors.

To build their nests, the eagles had also used what was at their disposal. Things like burial possessions, bone, hair, and clothing littered the massive structures.

The airborne creatures were actually living, breeding, and eating amongst the shredded carcasses of the tribes dead family members.

And before the horrified group of righteous believers could even get close enough to pear over its edge, many of the bald eagles furiously rose up and began to ferociously attack the intruders.

While some of the screaming banshees charged at them, others dove at the startled group and tried to rip apart clothing and any exposed flesh available.

If Hell had some way of vomiting its essence upon the land, this was definitely what one would have expected to see.

Beating back the extremely large birds that seemed to defy those trying to fend them off, Johnathon's congregation slowly began to advanced towards the cliffs edge.

And once there, they were horrified to find a small tribe of savages below.

In what the Protestant church considered pagan worship, the unsaved group who lived down there were placing their dead above them.

Yes, this is where they would face the giants.

It was now their responsibility to claim, settle, harvest, and partake of the land before them. Fertile terrain that was given to Johnathon and his devoted congregation by Yahweh himself.

Thus, saith god?

THUS, SAITH JONATHON.

CH 11.
WE COME IN PEACE.

Due to all the ruckus, it didn't take but a few minutes after the white ones were noticed before a partially naked group of stark raving mad natives appeared from below the ridge.

And as they began to fiercely approach them, Johnathon wasn't sure what to expect.

He has heard many fabled stories about how violent and savage these wildlings out west could be. Almost barbaric, were the reports spread from one wagging tongue to another.

Clearly, they had crossed some invisible line in the sand.

The Blessed Flock's leader knew, without a doubt, that if he did not act quickly it would be their flesh and bones resting in this place of purgatory.

Those that were approaching appeared to be almost frantic and completely out of control.

The tribe's men, while tripping over their own two feet, resembled little children trying to run for the very first time. And being carried in some of their hands were arrow ladened bows pulled back and aimed at every last one of them.

Others carried axes, spears, and hatchets.

Each one perfectly designed for stripping the flesh off their enemy's bones.

While shoving sharp jagged arrows into their rib sides, and any exposed flesh available, the people who lived down there continued to poke and prod at the intruding visitors in a frenzied pitch of anger and resentment.

With their freshly sharpened weapons waving in a motion that could easily have taken off a head, the first assembly of Harmony was forced to take a step back.

Father Johnathon's congregation was shoved far away from the ledge that overlooked an apple orchard growing in the valley below.

That's when the proclaimed Prophet, as if taken over by the Holy Spirit, very gracefully began speaking in inaudible tongues and was able to calmly back his flock away.

Somehow, do to his humbling and non-threatening manner, the pagans and everyone else began to follow his example.

And after being shoved another hundred or so feet away from the cliff's edge by the raging heathens, every male in the two different groups actually calmed down just enough to catch their breaths.

The natives could finally rest assured knowing that the sacred grounds of their ancestors was now safe and secure once again.

Without meaning too, they had just scared some lost god's descendants half to death.

Since the parishioners no longer stood upon the resting grounds of their ancestors, tribal elders quickly sized up the men, women, and children.

Standing before them in the morning's first light were the only white settlers any of them has ever seen.

The startled trespassers now appeared paler than before.

Local tribes were just starting to see and talk about these unnaturally tinctured settlers.

The bleached sun people had recently begun to pass through these parts as they made their way towards the westerly sea.

Most tended to travel a bit farther south.

But, wherever their God seemed to be leading them, they never bothered to take more than needed.

Thankfully, their kind never stayed long.

Hopefully, the ones camping above them will do the same.

These colorless ones, before moving on, were obviously needing some place to rest and obtain water. So, for now, the men had no fear that these frightened white people would purposely hurt, harm, or destroy them.

Without using their visitors Protestant words, the tribesmen gestured for the small group to rest, drink, and for the little while they would be here, do whatever was needed.

Now, after a full moons cycle had come to pass since the travelers first arrived, they were still camped out on the ridge above.

Something else had begun to camp out by the start of that next cycle of the moon too.

Dissention.

Do to the whispers about entire tribes being slaughtered, a few elders had begun to express their fears.

Because these accounts could not be verified firsthand, those in the valley below, for the most part, carried on as they have always done.

Before air, before water, before man was cast from the mud and women ripped from his side, they were.

Even before their ancestors walked upon this portion of the earth, the memories they shared farther back than time itself, says the tribe has always been and will always be.

As Harmony's Founding Father's with blood still freshly dripping from their hands, stood on the cliff above listening to the sounds coming from a dead and dying tribe, they began to shovel the pagan graveyard over the ridge and onto what was left of the tribal encampment below.

Then, just before the sun could fully rise above the scene of death and destruction, Harmony's Founding Fathers once again descended back into their valley and savagely suppressed the mourner's haunting song.

They needed to finish god's work before their wives, children, and the remaining residents of Harmony could possibly stir from their warm and snuggly beds.

The cicadas were also starting to snuggle into their long sleep of death below a blood-soaked ground in the apple orchard, when its soil began to reverberate from a mother's cry.

The Harpies shrilling screech wrapped around the cocoons so warm and cuddlesome that each one was rocked ever deeper into purgatory's darkened slumber.

But because of Harmony's Fathers, the lullaby that had tucked the earth's children to sleep in their cocooned caverns of hell was quickly silenced.

And it would be years before they heard her again.

After making sure the Fathers obeyed gods commandments, Pastor Johnathon must have sat amongst the dead on the valleys floor for over an hour before returning to his newly established town of Harmony.

The heavy clouds which had greeted Pastor Tucker at sunrise, now began to descend and blanket the valley below.

They were thicker than any east coast fog he has ever seen.

Thankfully, their deity was using them to hide those he and the Fathers had slaughtered from any prying eyes that might be eagerly tempted to peer over the cliffs edge.

Before heading home that day, Harmony's Founding Fathers were sworn to secrecy when it came to killing the women and children and ordered to never speak of their atrocities ever again.

Because of what was required to secure their place here on god's green earth, their families could never learn how much blood was spilt down in the valley below.

While ice cold water felt as if it were running through his veins, Johnathon never could bring himself to move from his spot at the cliffs edge.

As if he was one of those carved cigar Indians out in front of most general stores, he stood frozen for the remainder of that day and its entire night too.

There was no way he could go back down into the valley or return to his family until these clouds had lifted.

And even though he could no longer see who or what was down in the valley and caring on that haunting melody still crying in his ears, Pastor Tucker was not going to move one inch until he was completely certain that all the giants who had occupied their land were dead.

Then sometime around midnight, hours after everyone had finally returned to their dwellings, the heaviest of melted winter snows came sweeping through the valley.

God created a flash flood to purge the demons and their unholy filth from his sanctified land.

But Johnathon, like the Father's, were yet to see the Deities handywork. Because, like his son's resurrection, it wasn't until that third day, just after sunrise, before the Protestant's god finally lifted the veil from their shrouded valley.

All traces of its inhabitants, dwellings, eagle's, their nests, and tribal remains that had been dumped over the edge, were gone.

The only things left were the trees and a fresh layer of soil.

Because of their divine all mighty, the newly founded township could now prepare for their first apple harvest.

They had truly been blessed by their creator and believed that he was pleased with them for claiming and settling the land. God had, just for them and them only, specially set aside this garden of milk and honey.

Since he was the towns spiritual leader, it was now Father Johnathon's responsibility to bless the holy grounds for which god had provided.

And just as he was about to step onto the hidden trail leading down into the valley, a lone female child suddenly appeared out of nowhere and ended up slamming into him quite hard.

Their impact not only knocked the holy man off his feet, he brutally fell onto his back while the back of his head slammed against one of the footpaths larger boulders.

No!

This cannot be!

According to god, not one savage, not even a helpless child, may continue to live or breathe amongst his chosen few.

As Johnathon rapidly leapt up, what was left of the dissipating cloud bank began to swallow them both.

And while trying to grasp for the small child who was now doing everything she could to escape from his deadly grip, the thick soupy fog quickly hindered his vision.

His deity was making it utterly impossible for Harmony's Father to see what was going on around him.

Just as the almighty gave Abraham on order, trying the Fathers faith and seeing if he would actually kill his beloved son, Johnathon understood god was testing his heart and wondering if he would actually hunt down and kill the unholy spawn.

As he faithfully tried to capture the fleeing child, the closest thing within his grasp was her fringed leather tunic.

The bringer of death thought he might have blindly caught the tassels as his clenched fist gripped on tightly, but that thought and image in his head only lasted for a brief second or two.

And that's when the Devil decided to play a trick on him.

At first, the holy man couldn't comprehend what he was seeing.

The fog was just too thick.

It wasn't until his eyes finally adjusted to their grayish surroundings that Pastor Tucker suddenly realized clutched within his tightly clenched fist was an adolescent Eagle.

But what about the girl?

Where did she go?

Having just a few precious seconds to contemplate this mystery, Father Johnathon suddenly realized he was in a deadly predicament that would now require him to battle for his own life.

He and the great bird were firmly entangled.

As talons and hands began ripping and tearing at each other, the pair of predators danced a waltz of death along the trails edge.

About fifty-feet above the valleys floor.

Hoping that he could somehow beat the bird off, all Johnathon could do at this point was to try and defend himself. But the eagle had only one single purpose on its mind and one purpose only.

If it had anything to say about the destruction and killing of its nest and mate, this man's reckoning was going to end right here and right now.

Before it would be allowed to ascend, carrying the annihilated tribes vengeful prayers to their ancestors, the Great Spirit was given no choice but to leave its mark on this supposedly anointed individual.

Somewhere within its animalistic brain, while man and beast battled for dominance, the massive bird heard a commanding voice whisper these words.

An eye for an eye.

And because of the unforgivable acts that had occurred at the hands of this depraved soul, that's exactly what it was going to do.

As the raptor planted a firm and razor-sharp talon across his lower jaw, Pastor Tucker began to fathom what was about to take place.

Using its other free claw, the spiritual totem slammed its right foot across the Protestant teacher's skullcap and shoved his head backwards.

Johnathon was forced to look up at his god while the predator slammed its beak deep into his right eye.

After ripping the visual aid clean from the socket, like a fresh caught salmon, the savage bird opened its mouth, tossed back the peeper, and swallowed.

The vicious attack happened so quickly that Pastor Tucker had no time to pray or ask for help from his powerful god.

As he desperately tried to pry its claws from his face, the birds left talon now within Johnathon's death grip, had been grasped just firm enough that he was able to not only break it at the knee, he was able to rip it clean off the eagle.

If it had not been for gods miraculous strength flooding his spirit, because of Pastor Tucker's obedience, Johnathon understood that he could have possibly lost both eyes that day.

But, because of god's goodness and grace, he was still alive.

Thanks be to god.

Thus, saith god?

No.

Thus, Saith Johnathon?

Yes.

THUS, SAITH JOHNATHON.

The eagle no longer had a choice but to let go after losing its left talon, allowing man and beast to lick their wounds for another day, before ascending to the tribes ancestors with the last prayers his people had a chance to utter before they were all murdered by these soulless white invaders.

Kill them.

Kill them all.

******

CH 12.
A HOLY FATHER SINS.

After twelve long years, Johnathon couldn't believe that he was about to enter Harmony's apple orchard once again.

He had sworn many times over, that what had taken place in their valley was a price he had to pay for killing and destroying the Indians and their hallowed burial grounds.

They should never have been disturbed by him or Harmony's Founding Fathers.

Thus, Saith Johnathon?

THUS, SAITH GOD.

The tribal cries which had filled his soul back then, left their sorrow deep within Pastor Tuckers heart and mind.

And even though years have now passed, every single night since, they have continually haunted Jonathon's thoughts and dreams.

Not a day or hour has gone by that some faint whisper upon the wind hasn't caused Father Tucker's veins to fill with what felt like broken shards of glass to him.

Like the scalpel in a surgeon's skilled hands, his flesh felt like it was being skinned from the inside out.

Father Jonathon had fought long and hard not to hold Harmony's first Founders day down in the apple orchard. According to him, before their arrival, the trees would forever bless them with apples.

But now, their Pastor blatantly refused to propagate or plant the orchards trees upon Harmony's upper ridge.

Every single day he argued and cried till his voice was lost to rasping whispers of, please don't do this.

Don't plant the trees.

However, refusing to heed the Prophet's warnings, they went ahead and planted a few around the township anyway. They even went against their deities wishes and planted one upon the hallowed grounds of god's tabernacle.

Thus, Saith Johnathon?

THUS, SAITH GOD.

It was then, Father Johnathon decided to bar the doors to their little chapel.

And after locking himself inside, Pastor Tucker started carving his confession and the misdeeds he and the those who also committed the murderous atrocities with him.

Name, by name, by name.

Hopefully, these revelations would set Harmony's Fathers free from their genocidal lies.

Years ago, after the cleansing, Mary and Ruby Tucker had decided to pack a picnic lunch and wait for her pastoral husband to return from blessing their valley that day.

During that first storm, he stood watch over the orchard for an entire day and night.

His reasoning was to make sure that everyone would be safe to settle, live, and farm the blessed area from any of those who might have escaped god's righteous wrath.

Pagan worshipers who never should have entered the deities garden in the first place.

They were just in the wrong spot at the wrong time.

Oopsie.

Now, bow your heads and repeat after me.

Dear Lord, what have we done?

Pastor Tucker was the first and only one to enter their valley that morning.

So, when Jonathon returned around one that afternoon, he was not only white as a ghost and covered from head to foot in blood, the frazzled Saint kept repeating the same phrase over, and over, and over.

Their gone.

Their gone.

Their gone.

They're are really gone.

Before the injured husband quickly shuffled past Mary and Ruby on his way towards their eastwardly facing makeshift church that was built so its congregation, leader, and alter all faced the divine's glorious throne.

That way, if god so chose to speak to his blessed flock, he would tell Johnathon first and the incorruptible Prophet will tell us.

Wouldn't he?

Yes.

Yes he would.

Thus, saith god?

No.

Thus, Saith Johnathon?

No.

Thus, saith god and Johnathon?

No.

Thus Saith Johnathon and god?

No.

Thus, Saith He who speaks to god?

Yes.

THUS, SAITH THE PROPHET.

Now, bow your heads and repeat after me.

Dear Lord, what have we done?

Eventually, they were planning on replacing the four posted tent and its canopied top with a more permanent structure.

As the seriously injured leader entered the newly erected tabernacle his family and the towns radical belief system were currently housed in, June Windgood, who was there to spread some fresh hay before that evenings service, instantly knew something very serious had happened to the Father.

From the holy man's crown, down to his blessed feet, every inch of clothing and exposed flesh was ripped, shredded, and dripping in blood.

Her battered and bloodied Prophet kind of reminded the midwife of a bloodletting appointment going horribly wrong because it was perform by an overzealous doctor.

You see, today just happens to be your lucky day.

You're his first patient ever.

And by the way, try not to move while I cut you.

Torture was more like it.

And the only reason that image popped into the recent convert's thoughts was due to the insistence of June's Mother that she read a book describing the church's horrible actions during those plagued dark ages.

As a young girl, she learned about the viciously made up lies church leaders propagated just so they could pillage, rape, and murder at will.

Their fanatical abusers, the Church.

So, some of the opposing team decided to change their name, pack their shit, and leave.

According to those who witnessed the altercation firsthand, the cultist heretics last and final words were, you and your pope can kiss our Protestant ass.

And because of their devoted faith, obedience to act, and willingness to believe in every word the Prophet has to say, he who consecrates and watches over his chosen leader led the Blessed Flock to this abandoned grove of Apples.

Seems the deity was going to try and create perfection one last time.

And, according to our leader, Pastor Johnathon Tucker, this is the exact spot where the Prophet and his flock are supposed to start all over again while the rest of mankind gets slowly devoured by their lustful pursuits for objects that never satisfy our lecherous flesh.

So, to keep that from happening to us, we packed-up everything we owned and left.

And then, just like Johnathon prophesied, we stumbled upon this unoccupied piece of parcel.

Thus, saith god?

No.

Thus, Saith Johnathon?

No.

Thus, saith god and Johnathon?

No.

Thus, Saith Johnathon and god?

No.

Thus, Saith He who speaks to god?

Yes.

THUS, SAITH THE PROPHET.

Now, bow your heads and repeat after me.

Dear Lord, what have we done?

Since his face was shrouded by a pair of shredded appendages; the moment Father Johnathon stumbled into the tent, Sister Windgood could see that some of his injuries looked to be quite severe.

So, without a minute to waist, June quickly gathered Harmony's Protestant women together for a moment of silent prayer.

With their hands grasped tightly in fear, the shaky prayer group began to cry out to their deity.

The baker's dozen were compelling Mr. Almighty to intervein on their behalf .

The Protestant worshipers were feverishly asking the creator of all things to grant them the faith and courage needed while hesitantly shuffling towards the ledge were the eagles once lived and nested.

An inaccessible outcropping that used to be covered with wagon sized roosts made from twigs, bone, and weaponry, while plastered in layers of feathers and rotting flesh.

All topped with a large helping of smeared goodness.

Vomit, piss, and shit.

And from the looks and size of it all, the heathen invaders appear to have been living and worshiping like this for a long, long time.

And now, according to the Prophet, god said it's high time they left.

Thus, saith god?

No.

Thus, Saith Johnathon?

No.

Thus, saith god and Johnathon?

No.

Thus, Saith Johnathon and god?

No.

Thus, Saith He who speaks to god?

Yes.

THUS, SAITH THE PROPHET.

Now, bow your heads and repeat after me.

Dear Lord, what have we done?

As their god-forsaken Idols were being built, a person could easily tell the fiercely opposing predator constructed these impressive abodes with whatever sticks and twigs that could be flown in from other locations.

The large convocation numbering around thirty or so, were also using the things that just so happened to be left by those who fed and cared for the aerial spirits along the treeless ridge.

While troves of weaponry lay scattered across the well sized outcropping, things like axes, bows, spears and clothing were internally woven within their templatic idolatry too.

Then, to top off all that madness, the skeletal remains of fish, small birds, and an occasional fox, rabbit, or squirrel, also littered a number of the love dens where juvenile fledglings were still testing out their wings and boundaries.

These unsightly areas of witchery were then patched together with flesh that was still rotting, animal waste that was still decomposing, and feathers.

Oh the feathers!

Like temple converts trapped in a frenzied dance of worship, the entire area, extending at least fifty feet from the ledge, flowed and swayed with the creatures plumage.

And it was good.

Thus, saith god?

No.

Thus, Saith Johnathon?

No.

Thus, saith god and Johnathon?

No.

Thus, Saith Johnathon and god?

No.

Thus, Saith He who speaks to god.

Yes.

THUS, SAITH THE PROPHET.

Now, bow your heads and repeat after me.

Dear Lord, what have we done?

In the past, if any of the Prophet's children wished to peak over its edge, they would need to walk through an unholy place of Idolatry worship.

So, like cancer, god immediately realized that it needed to be cut out or the infection will spread and he will have to destroy everything and start over once again.

And to their astonishment, while sheepishly peering together over the cliff, all traces of the village and those who had lived there were gone.

Not one stick or stone that had been stacked upon the other, was left.

It was all gone.

Just gone.

Now, bow your heads and repeat after me.

Dear Lord, what have we done?

And by the time Harmony's townsfolk were ready for bed, word had quickly spread from wife to husband that god had descended from his throne hidden amongst the clouds and wiped away all the blemishes from their sacred land.

The deity had even blessed them all by taking away those awful remains of the heathen's corpses and birds with him.

Truly, their congregation was meant to be here.

So that very next day, after calling their entire town together, they unanimously agreed to remember this victory as Founders Day.

Hear after, it would-be set-in stone that upon every Founders Day, no matter what, they had to do something special for Father Johnathon, the Founding Fathers, and their township.

Thus, saith god?

No.

Thus, Saith Johnathon?

No.

Thus, saith god and Johnathon?

No.

Thus Saith Johnathon and god?

No.

Thus, Saith He who speaks to god?

No.

Thus, Saith the Blessed Flock?

Yes.

THUS, SAITH THE BLESSED FLOCK.

Now, bow your heads and repeat after me.

Dear Lord, what have we done?

Thankfully, the flood that swept their valley clean ended up leaving all of the apple trees untouched.

The river had not only left its thick rich soil, but it also filled the trees buds with fresh, untainted mountain water also. This blessing would cause the delectable fruit to be the fattest and juiciest apples in that entire area.

Yes, this truly was a land flowing with milk and honey.

And when it came time to harvest those sweet, sweet apples; from here on out, they would hold Harmony's celebrations down in the valley's grove.

Every year before the festivities could begin, the Founder's heroic story would be told and retold.

According to legendary tales, without the Father's lifting a single finger, the Prophet's unassisted hand had wiped across the valley floor and cleansed their blessed orchard from those godless savages.

The prognosticator's fervent prayers moved god so much, the diviner washed away all the evil from their promised land on the Prophet and his blessed flocks behalf.

This was the vision god had given to Father Tucker right before they packed up and left the Church.

A faithful and sinless man unlike those who used to live here.

When he hurriedly strode past the congregation's women the day he was almost killed, Jonathon had no doubt that all the blood had drained from his face.

As Pastor Tucker approached their newly erected tent they were temporarily using for church services, Father Jonathon knew no one would approach, challenge, or bother him this evening because of the current state he was in.

In fact, no one dared to say a word until he decided to come back out and make his presence known.

The Protestant Preacher always felt that when god wanted to speak with him in person, all he had to do was find a bible and see were the pages randomly fell open.

However, this day its spiritual inspiration would be just a little harder to read.

Thus, saith god?

Thus, Saith Johnathon.

PROVERBS 20:18

HE THAT COVERETH HIS SINS SHALL NOT PROSPER: BUT HE WHO SO CONFESSETH AND FORSAKETH THEM ALL, SHALL HAVE EVER LASTING MERCY.

And now, seventeen years later, just as they were beginning to celebrate another Founders Day, Father Jonathon, hoping Harmony's towns folk would finally listen and take him seriously, forced himself to enter the orchard.

It was a reception the Fathers were not overwhelmed to see him partake of.

There stood the unbathed Prophet clothed in apple sacks.

And by the smell of him, it was pretty obvious months have passed since the religious leader's unwashed body has been anywhere near a tub of soapy water.

Apple branches had been tied around his waist for a belt.

He was also sporting over his missing oculus an eyepatch made from dried apple skins.

All the while critically denouncing every last Father there.

The crazy and lying lunatic was spouting scripture condemning their heinous actions and refusing to partake in the Founding celebrations of Harmony.

Seems the Prophet had a change of heart about this place after he was attacked by the eagle and eventually lost his ever-loving mind.

According to Johnathon, He, the Fathers and the Blessed Flock had sinned and were no longer allowed to be here.

A retraction everyone ignored because there was no way they were willfully going to leave this place on their own accord after putting in seventeen years of backbreaking work.

And now, seeing how he was dressed, they did agree on one thing.

The townsfolk no longer had any qualms about who was the one needing to leave after realizing their beloved Pastor has finally flipped his rocker.

The wagon train has derailed, ladies and gentleman.

I repeat, the wagon train has derailed.

There had been occasions in Pastor Jonathon's leadership, when he taught that certain people were to be shunned for their sinful behavior.

For the salvation of that person's soul, his congregation was ordered to follow suit.

If someone wasn't working hard enough, sharing food, or paying their tithes, then, "according to Pastor Tucker," they were nothing but a wolf hiding in sheep's clothing.

Let the shunning begin.

This time, it was the Founding Fathers who single handedly forced Harmony's residents to turn away from their fallen leader.

Thus, Saith Johnathon?

NO!

Thus, saith god?

NO!

Thus, Saith the Fathers?

YES!

Now, bow your heads and repeat after us.

Dear Lord, what have we done?

Like a starving vulture after being run off from its decaying meal-ticket, the madman sat on the cliffs edge behind Harmony's new church overlooking the grove and its festivities.

And as he continued to watch the celebrations, their Holy man, unbeknownst to those below, now stared down into the valley with an ever-growing hunger for their righteous judgment.

To hide any and all evidence of their genocidal crimes, the Father's made sure to build their Protestant Sanctuary right on top of the area were the Indian burial grounds used to be.

A stupid move on their part.

And the Prophet reminded them of that every chance he got.

Even today, on this most Holy of days, the uninvited guest showed up and started spouting off his deceptions once again.

And the Father's were tired of it.

They, and those partaking of the joyful merriment unanimously agreed that Pastor Tucker was no longer welcomed and needed to leave before the Fathers could physically respond and toss his ass out.

This was a joyful day of remembrance for all the sacrifices and hardships Harmony's Founders had to face just to find this magical place.

The Fathers nor the Blessed Flock were going to quietly stand back and allow Johnathon and his unkept presence to tarnish or bring a bad spirit of witchcraft and unfounded lies to such hallowed commemorations.

Thus, Saith Johnathon?

NO!

Thus, saith god?

NO!

Thus, Saith the Fathers?

YES!

THUS, SAITH THE FATHERS!

Now, bow your heads and repeat after us.

Dear Lord, what have we done?

While Johnathon continued to sit there, it soon occurred to him that the cicadas had started to hatch and were beginning to overrun their unholy valley.

Once again, the shrilling insects penetrating cries caused the very ground Father Tucker sat upon to vibrate from the Siren's mind-numbing melody.

Never in Johnathon's life has he had such a tormenting headache like the one he is currently dealing with.

Never in his life has he experienced this kind of blinding rage.

And, never in his life has he had such contentious hate for those he vowed to keep safe and out of harm's way.

Except for his wife and daughter, Mary and Ruby Beth, Johnathon knew that he would eventually have to expose the sins of Harmony's Founding Fathers.

Even if that meant killing them using his own flesh clawed hands.

CH 13.
CRAZY, I'M CRAZY FOR BEING SO BLUE.

Somewhere in the back of Pastor Tuckers unhinged mind, where murderous thoughts swarmed with contempt for every soul around him, a dark nursery rhyme began to whisper its unpleasantries.

And as the blood lust began to boil and overtake the God-fearing Pastor; from somewhere deep down within the holy man's suppressed memories a familiar tune began to unconsciously join the broken symphony forming in his fractured mind.

Its melodious melody and suggestive lyrics began to weave their influential suggestions amongst the crazy man's homicidal thoughts.

Johnathon really loved the way his tongue vibrated as he began to croon to its musical perfection.

Its tonal quality was quite pleasing to his pallet.

Almost as if a Cicada had decided to crawl into his mouth so that it could talk with he who speaks to god.

Buzz, buzz, buzz?

Buzz, Buzz.

BUZZZZZZZ.

BUZZZZZZZ.

BUZZ AROUND THE ROSY.

A POCKET FULL OF POSIES.

BUZZ, BUZZ.

BUZZ, BUZZ.

THEY ALL DIE NOW!

What was supposed to be the best Founders Day ever, nature quickly turned into a natural disaster.

Because of the lies, disobedience, and murderous actions committed by the Founding Fathers at the hands of a false Prophet, God decided it was finally time to punish all of Harmony's deceitful residents.

Children included.

Ready or not, the Deity was going to do it using the eighth plague of Egypt.

And that judgment begins now.

Thus, Saith the Blessed Flock?

YES.

Thus, Saith the Fathers?

YES.

Thus, Saith Johnathon?

YES.

And, Thus Saith the God called Ra.

His Holy Prophet too.

Hear what they have to say.

And do as they do.

Now, bow your heads and pray to he.

Call upon Ra and he will call upon thee.

Shout his name.

One, two, three.

RA!

RA!

RA!

Down in the apple orchard of Hades, the entire brood of the noisy insectoids had finally bored their way through Harmony's blood soaked underground.

Unbeknownst to most of the town's residents, the grove is where the bug seasonally rested in an eternal torment amongst the buried and undiscovered remains of the areas former natives.

All killed by the Founding Father's own hands.

And after committing that atrocity, the men tried to cover their crimes by burying everyone underneath a pile of nests large enough to pass as a debris filled beaver dam that had been washed downstream during a flashflood.

So, because there was nothing special about the dam.

And being told not to give a dam.

No one touched the dam.

No one went to the dam.

No one even looked at the dam.

It's just a god-damned dam.

Thankfully, there was no need for that excuse because the damned dam washed away before anyone had a chance to see it.

Within hours of the failed festivities, Harmony's entire valley, from river to mountain top, had been so overrun with the cicada's incessive mating call that it caused Johnathon and his dementias brain to violently throb from their reverberating madness.

The screeching wails from the maddened banshees were so overwhelming that those involved in the festivities didn't just pack up and leave in peace that day, they didn't pack up at all.

Instead, Harmony's squatters ran screaming from the garden.

It was as if their very lives depended on how fast they could flee.

Without giving it a second thought, unpacked or not, every last picnic basket, serving dish, utensils, skillets, and jars, was instantaneously abandoned.

And not one single item was ever retrieved again.

Probably because their rightful owners were never brave enough to enter the winged cauldron of boiling death and retrieve them.

Buzz, Buzz, Buzz?

Buzz, Buzz.

BUZZZZZZZ.

BUZZZZZZZ.

Now, bow your heads and pray to he.

Call upon Ra and he will call upon thee.

Shout his name.

One, two, three.

RA!

RA!

RA!

As Father Johnathon quietly sat there watching the insanity below, seemingly lost in the presence of God, he quickly became mesmerized by the cicada's psalms and dance.

That entire day, and throughout the following weeks, Father Jonathon, while praying and fasting, remained steadfast on the cliffs edge behind their House of Worship.

He was fully immersed by the cicada's hypnotic hymn and reveling on their every last note.

Buzz, Buzz, Buzz?

Buzz, Buzz.

BUZZZZZZZ.

BUZZZZZZZ.

Now, bow your heads and pray to me.

Call upon Ra and I will call upon thee.

Shout my name.

One, two, three.

RA!

RA!

RA!

According to the Prophet, the cicadas were bereaving.

They were not just looking for a mate, the pesky critters were also searching and calling out for the return of their Earthly Mother.

She had excruciatingly lamented them into deaths snuggling velvet slumber many years ago.

It had been such a soothing experience.

The insects wanted their future offspring, before mating season ended, to partake in the same blessings of flesh and blood like they had.

Its fiery touch had soothingly satisfied their long, long slumber.

So, from that very first heartbeat to its last breath, the cicadas living and breeding in that valley unceasingly offered up their screeching melody.

They were hoping Mother Earth would somehow hear her offspring's cry and return once again.

Just as they were sang to sleep, the rambunctious Cicadidae wanted this next generation to be lulled into the afterlife within her warm and bloody embrace too.

And they were not the only ones.

Like the aerial projectiles, Harmony's Prophet was starting to feel that way also.

Kill them.

Kill them all.

BUZZZZZZZ.

BUZZZZZZZ.

Now, bow your heads and pray to me.

Call upon Ra and I will call upon thee.

Shout my name.

One, two, three.

RA!

RA!

RA!

The congregation was pretty sure, especially after four weeks of just sitting there, that Pastor Jonathon had finally slipped into madness.

For that entire duration, no one has personally seen him eat or move from behind their church.

And when the time came to take a piss or shit, he never seemed to move for that knock on the door either.

While continually whispering and snickering to himself in a giddy, possessed kind of way, the man just sat there rocking back and forth in his own maddened filth.

Day, after day, after day.

For those who were brave enough to approach and still willing to believe and hear the Prophet out, he had a warning from God.

And they damned well better listen because it wasn't good.

Thus, Saith God.

A WITCH IS COMING.

TO TEAR DOWN THE HOUSE.

UNRIGHTEOUSLY BUILT.

>   WITH GOD'S RIGHTEOUS CLOUT.
>
>   A WITCH IS COMING.
>
>   TO TEAR DOWN THE HOUSE.
>
>   UNRIGHTEOUSLY BUILT.
>
>   WITH GOD'S RIGHTEOUS CLOUT.
>
>   A WITCH IS COMING.
>
>   TO TEAR DOWN THE HOUSE.
>
>   UNRIGHTEOUSLY BUILT.
>
>   WITH GOD'S RIGHTEOUS CLOUT.

Thus, saith the Blessed Flock?

No.

Thus, saith Johnathon?

NO.

Thus, saith the Fathers?

NO.

Thus, Saith God?

YES!

THUS, SAITH GOD!

Now, bow your heads and pray to me.

Call upon Ra and I will call upon thee.

Shout my name.

One, two, three.

RA!

RA!

RA!

Really people?

That shit show is your doing, not mine.

Because the town's residents ended up trapped in their houses do to the swarming plague of cicadas, Harmony's men had become easily angered and violent.

No matter how minuscule the bickering, every single disagreement eventually broke out into a physical altercation.

And once the arguments got started between husbands, wives, and children, its outcome always ended the exact same way.

SMACK!

Violent disagreements, (SMACK), usually caused by discussing the early retirement of a certain individual who shall not be named.

SMACK!

The conundrum of what to do with their fallen leader.

Pastor Jonathon Tucker.

He had prophesied that by gods hand, and god's hand only, the deity would completely wipe away all traces of those native savages from their blessed land.

When this divine intervention actually occurred, it proved beyond a shadow of a doubt that Father Johnathon definitely has gods ear.

But does he still, the townsfolk pondered.

The now exalted Prophet Tucker, and Prophet Tucker alone, seems to have been given Gods righteous indignation and was unquestionably able to speak and act on the Deity's behalf.

He, in the eyes of God and his Blessed Flock was without a doubt an actual Prophet.

But, back then he wasn't bat shit crazy like he is now.

That person out there is no longer the man they once knew.

Just looking at the disheveled state he was currently in, the Blessed Flock deduced that the Holy Father appears to have fallen from grace.

So, Harmony's residents finally decided it was their responsibility to do something about it since god didn't appear to be interested in doing anything with his broken toy.

The Prophet must be killed.

If every congregant stands in agreement, let the Blessed Flock raise their hands and say so.

All in favor?

So.

Now, bow your heads and repeat after your Fathers.

Dear Lord, what have we done?

As the sun was just beginning to set, Harmony's Holy Fathers quietly gathered together and tried to retrieved Pastor Tucker from behind their little white church.

But, to their shock and horror, the congregational leaders did not find a whole man.

Instead, the shocked Protestant Inquisitors found the Prophet completely nude and drenched from head to foot in his own blood.

The Founders tried their best to keep the Pastor's horrendous state from their women and children, but that was never going to happen.

As they slowly approached the bloody man who was barely recognizable to any of them now, it quickly became pretty obvious that he was not going into their now forsaken orchard willingly.

If they wished to shove him down the steep and narrow ledge, and because he gave them no other choice, Johnathan would have to be tied up first.

And the winged bugs seemed to have an issue with that death-penalty resolution.

As their mournful wailing continually grew louder and louder that day, the entire valley made a perfect acoustical stage for the cicada's resonating echoes.

Every structure, resident, and inch of flesh in Harmony seemed to rhythmically reverberate in sync with the cicada's invasive cry.

Its goose pimpled effect also caused every hair on the human body to stand straight up.

And once that happened, the apple trees that had been planted around the township began acting like tuning forks.

The air itself seemed to come alive as it ebbed and flowed with cicadas and their feverishly pitched composition of insanity.

There wasn't even room enough to go outside and breathe.

Without crushing a few here or there, their uncountable numbers also made it completely impossible to do anything.

The moment someone tried, the suffocating insects would go straight for the airways. A few of Harmony's residents actually dropped dead because they couldn't catch a breath.

They were everywhere.

Their molted shells lain strewn across every inch of ground, every screen or fence, every car, and tree.

Just exiting and entering an exterior door felt like a game of Russian Roulette. In the few seconds that life-raft was opened just wide enough to slip through, hundreds of the buggers would get in.

And even if you were somehow able to ignore that fact, it always felt as if they were out to kill you during the process of trying to accomplish whatever mundane errand needed completing when headed outside.

And now, because of Pastor Tucker's insane actions, he and Harmony's Protestant Leaders were headed into the pit of Hell were the invasive insects madness first started.

When it comes to the good book, "according to the Prophet," before a Holy Man and his Blessed Flock can stand in the presence of God, they must first be covered in prayer and repented of their sins.

A commandment Harmony's Founders have yet to fulfill.

But all of that was about to change thanks to God's Prophet.

As the Father's continued down the path, the frightened men put in charge of guarding the deranged preacher observed that their fallen prophet had carved biblical scriptures anywhere he could have possibly reached.

It was quite unnerving.

Every available surface of his nude body had been clawed and ripped apart with the talon of a juvenile eagle.

And, he was still in possession of the deadly implement.

Do to the death grip Johnathon had on the claw, the Fathers were unable, and definitely unwilling, to try and pry it from his blood-stained hands.

So, to keep from playing a game of duck, duck, goose; you're it, they unanimously decided to just let him walk down with it.

Really, just look at him, what harm is he to any of us now?

But he was.

And the Prophet knew it.

The Deity was not finished with them just yet.

Just as Cain was cursed for killing Abel, the sinners were about to be punished for their own murderous actions.

All of them.

Men, women, and children alike.

Even if that meant Johnathon had to take matters into his own hands once again.

Before it was said, done, and over with, God's chosen Prophet was going to make sure, for their own salvation, Harmony's Founders were going to pay for their sinful actions.

One way, or another.

Buzz, Buzz, Buzz?

Buzz, Buzz.

BUZZZZZZZ.

BUZZZZZZZ.

Now, bow your heads and pray to me.

Call upon Ra and I will call upon thee.

Shout my name.

One, two, three.

RA!

RA!

RA!

CH 14.
STICKS AND STONES BREAK BONES.

It had to be the screeching cicadas from their apple orchard that was the cause of his and everyone else's violent outburst.

After months of the critters never-ending wails, their nerves were definitely shot.

So, who could blame them for losing their minds?

Only their all-forgiving Lord knows the number of unaccounted instances each Father, (SMACK, SMACK), ended up sending wives and children flying across a dimly lit room.

That first, (SMACK), of the day usually came from either the fist, (SMACK), back of his hand, (SMACK), or boot, (SMACK).

Homicidal rages, (SMACK, SMACK, SMACK), that were profitably applied to every exposed area available.

As the blinding anger and blood red fog filled a Father's every thought and action towards their frightened families and friends, it soon became apparent that it was just best for everyone to look away and mind their own damned business when the head of their household did.

SMACK!

SMACK!

SMACK!

A decision those trapped inside with their abusers highly disagreed with.

SMACK!

After shaking off a fit of rage, the men had lost count over how many times they awoke from the madness only to find the house in disarray and their beaten and blooded family cowering in the corner.

The women had lost count over how many times, (SMACK), they found daddies calloused hands placed firmly around their choking throats.

And, according to the children, they had also lost count over how many times they awoke to find those who shared his bed and home, imprisoned by his utter hate and distain for them.

SMACK!

SMACK!

SMACK!

SMACK!

SMACK!

Really, how many times in a day can a wife, (SMACK), or children, (SMACK) be screamed, kicked, or beat upon.

SMACK!

The regularly abused women who had timidly watched from behind closed shutters as their husbands disappeared into the night, were glad for the reprieve.

Because, for now, even if their husband's absence only lasted a few hours, the tortured families gratefully watched them walk into the evenings quickly darkening twilight.

The time had finally come to do something about their tormenting predicament.

By setting the orchard on fire, Harmony's men were not only going to burn those demonic insects out, but Pastor Tucker needed to be physically dealt with also.

And then came the darkness.

As each Father headed down that single file trail, how could the entourage have known that within a matter of seconds they would quickly lose sight of the others.

The unexpected vail of fog they were now stumbling within was thicker than any of the men had ever experienced.

Not even the torches firelight could pierce through the blanket of total darkness that an all-consuming and undeniable deity had tucked around them like a warm blanket.

The ninth plague of Egypt was now upon them.

Unbeknownst to his captors, Johnathon, with god's blessing, was going to see to it that they were all going to answer for their sinful actions.

And as the valley's apple covered grounds loomed closer and closer, the time to act had finally arrived.

Buzz, Buzz, Buzz?

Buzz, Buzz.

BUZZZZZZZ.

BUZZZZZZZ.

Now, bow your heads and pray to me.

Call upon Ra and I will call upon thee.

Shout my name.

One, two, three.

RA!

RA!

RA!

Do to the fact that Harmony's Fathers wanted to get this done and over with, the distances between them began to increase at a sick and quickening pace.

The Holy men couldn't even hear each other cry out when it came to a safety check because the cicadas were so overbearingly loud.

Buzz, Buzz, Buzz?

Buzz, Buzz.

BUZZZZZZZ.

BUZZZZZZZ.

Before setting their blessed orchard on fire, the Protestant Forbearers had decided to go down amongst the apple trees and somehow reason with Pastor Jonathon.

And, if left with no other options, they would, (SMACK), beat the madness right out of him.

The last time any of the towns leadership were here, was when those infernal insects sent everyone fleeing like a pack of mischief rats trying not to drown as the ship sinks.

A survival instinct that was now being tossed aside.

Other than a crazy Prophet, their next greatest fear was that Hell's demons had been set free and were slithering amongst the cicada infested valley below.

When the Founders saw their drenched in blood Rector mutilating himself, they finally accepted the undeniable fact Pastor Jonathon had to be put down.

So, before he could possibly harm their own precious women and children just as they had, the Prophet's demise needed to be immediately dealt with.

Not one Father wanted to verbally admit that he feared Johnathon would certainly kill them before he could be escorted to the orchard.

So, as they continued on their way, Harmony's Fathers began to loudly pray for god's guiding hand concerning the deity's laws and what to do about his heretic Prophet.

They were begging, bartering, and pleading for Mr. All-knowing to intercede on their behalf because no one really wished to discipline someone god should have taken care of the very minute their Holy Reverend's cuckoo clock first ticked.

And Ra agreed.

He was more than willing to answer their deceitful prayers.

Every last one of them.

But, before he does, god just needed to consult with the Prophet first.

Buzz, Buzz, Buzz?

Buzz, Buzz.

BUZZZZZZZ.

BUZZZZZZZ.

It's time to repent, Tucker giggled with glee.

Now, bow your heads and pray to he.

Call upon Ra and he will call upon thee.

Shout his name.

One, two, three.

RA!

RA!

RA!

When that last man stepped onto the valley floor, Johnathon struck out with his eagle's talon and ripped out the throat of the Father standing closest to him.

His quick and deadly actions instantaneously sent that elder collapsing into the thick, mist covered ground of Hades.

And no one saw a thing.

The Prophet's first strike made it completely impossible for him to warn any of the other Fathers of what was happening because he was drowning in the pints of blood that were now draining into the man's slashed windpipe.

Unlike the horrors that were imagined while the solemn group descended the orchards steep path, Hells demons did not slither amongst its shadowed possibilities.

Instead, the creature crawled, ran, and tore the very last breath from the deceivers.

Their dead and stone-cold hearts actually believed what they had done, "according to Father Johnathon's insistence," was the right thing to do.

Each Founder had sworn an oath to the others, if what they did was ever spoken of again, god, "and only god," was the one who sent the flash flooding rains that ended up washing away the savage's and their village.

But once he survived the Eagle's attack, Johnathon suddenly had a change of heart concerning his misgivings about the Earth Children.

And after years of repentance and self-reflection, the Prophet finally understood the Fathers would never admit or ask God to forgive them for their blood-thirsty sins.

It was such an evil thing to do that night.

And Cain was about to do it again.

Because the Protestant Leaders were refusing to follow the Prophets example, Johnathon decided to hunt every single one of them down.

It seemed to him, after all these years, the only way their deceitful tongues were going to be set free was for God's Holy

Messenger to personally slit those sinful throats and sprinkle the alter with the Father's grisly entrails.

A horrendous action the burrowing bugs were grateful for.

Finally, after the Father's blood began to soak deep into Harmony's orchard, the cicadas cried out for the mother once more.

They, just as the Father's, were ready to take that last breath and die.

Whether their rock-a-by slumber would be a peaceful one or not was now up to the mother. Thankfully, the burrowing Auchenorrhyncha wouldn't have to wait long.

Just after sunrise, the wives of Harmony's Founding Fathers slowly awoke to empty beds.

The Protestant women joyfully realized that they were actually able to sleep in and had awakened to a calm and peaceful dawn.

For the first time, in a long time, they would be able to start their day without a husbands, (SMACK), or having to listen to him beating on the children's door while trying quite successfully, "the housewives would add," to get everyone motivated for the start of a new day.

That first, (SMACK), of the day usually occurred before the cock had a chance to crow.

Finally, someone upstairs cared enough to answer their prayers.

And even though they were all ecstatic being able to begin the day without an opened palm slap to their faces, (SMACK), somewhere deep within their twisted, gut-wrenching belly's, the wives knew someone had to go out and look for the missing Founders.

That someone turned out to be them.

Hopefully, they were not down in the apple grove still.

So, just after they had a chance to cook, eat breakfast, and do the dishes, with Harmony's remnants by their side for support and protection, the women, children, and what few elderly men remained, hesitantly locked hands and began their descent into the shrouded grove.

For the first time in months, the air was not only still, but so, so quiet.

As they began to look around with an overpowering dread of foreboding, most were sure that every Brothers Grimm fairytale, told by the firelight was about to come true.

And what had the Fathers done with Pastor Tucker?

The orchard was still thick with fog and the stench of kerosene from their burnt-out torches hung heavily upon its mist.

If the hand of death had any weight, it could not have been any heavier than the unseen horror that unexpectedly awaited the town's residents.

Boogeymen and all scary tales told about unholy things which kill at their discretion, filled the minds of every woman, child, and those who had been brave enough to accompany them into the orchard.

Once again, Harmony's prayers were about to be answered by their god.

As the investigative group began to shuffle ever so hesitantly into the stand of trees, Harmony's Founding Fathers appeared to be hanging out underneath the garden's main attraction.

But, because the Blessed Flock's view was being obscured by a thick blanket of fog, it was almost impossible to tell what the Father's were doing.

And it wasn't until they got just a bit closer that their inquisitive questions were answered.

Here in this blessed land flowing with milk and honey, were their husbands. Someone had hung them underneath the Grandfather of Pome fruits.

As that first breeze of the morning started to blow, their lifeless bodies began to sway ever so gently.

Not only had their throats been slit, but the carcasses had also been gutted from the crack of their ass to their voice box.
They appeared to have been hung from the apple tree with their own entrails.

And there in the mist, crouching underneath the dead men was god's chosen Prophet.

Pastor Johnathon Tucker.

He was soaked from head to foot with the bloody remnants from Harmony's Fathers and what little remained of his shredded flesh.

In his clenched hands was an eagle's talon.

Everywhere the Holy man could possibly have reached, looked as if he had tried to rip the flesh from his own body.

So, as the Fathers wives began to beat their breast, wailing that beautiful, mournful song of death over Harmony's blood-soaked grounds, the cicada's children began their slumbering death to a mother's cry.

Buzz, Buzz, Buzz?

Buzz, Buzz.

BUZZZZZZ.

BUZZZZZZ.

ABOUT THE AUTHOR.

Writer E.A. Green/The Greenman is a former resident of Rockport, Texas and currently lives in the small rural town of Erick, Oklahoma.

His prolific library now consist of 16 books.

Dawn of the Cicada, Curse of the Cicada, Song of the Cicada, Death of the Cicada, The Prophet, The Prodigal, The Blessed Flock, Flesheaters, Father May I, Real Skin, Delta Dawn, Just Jellies, and Wake the Dead, Tales of Madness and Mayhem.

This unique storyteller also has a children's series called Don't Let the Bedbugs Bite.

Book one is titled, Don't Let the Bedbugs Bite.

Part 2 is titled Critters, Jitters, and Shivers.

While Part 3 goes by Ooey, Gooey, and Chewy.

Currently, E.A. Green is associated with Jack in the Green Publishing.

His literary accomplishments can also be found at Amazon and other places such as Barnes & Nobles.

All novellas and short stories can also be found, requested, or ordered through your towns library system.

The next classic to be joining his children's series is titled Bedbugs 4, Jiggly, Squiggly, and Wiggly.

Look for it and his newest novel, SVNTxSVN, sometime in the fall of 2023 to late spring of 2024.

213

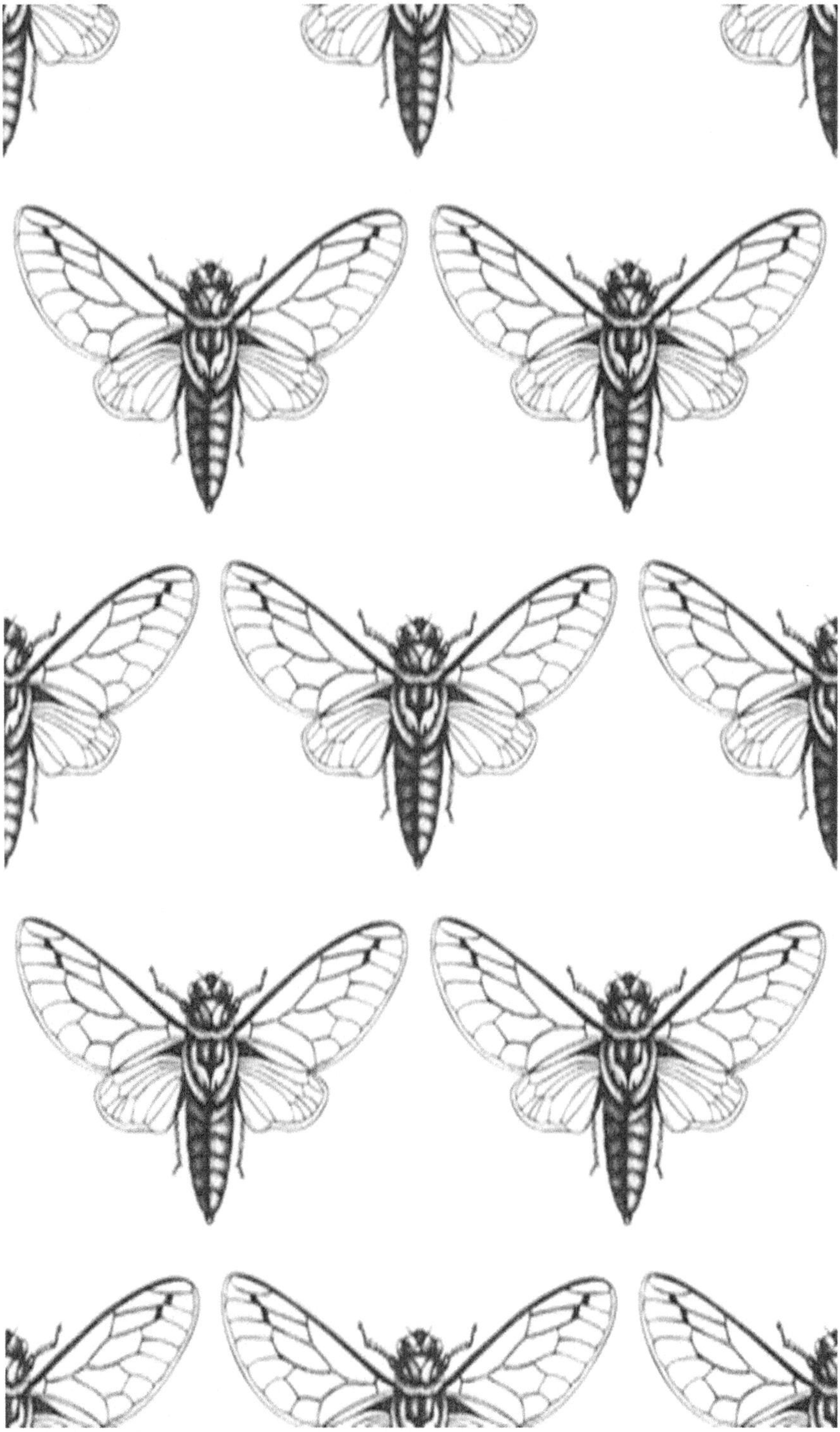

Made in the USA
Columbia, SC
19 July 2024